Magic Puppy

Books 1-2

SUE BENTLEY

illustrated by Angela Swan

Grosset & Dunlap

GROSSET & DUNLAP
An Imprint of Penguin Random House LLC, New York

Text copyright © 2008 by Sue Bentley. Illustrations copyright © 2008 by
Angela Swan. Cover illustrations copyright © 2008 by Andrew Farley.
A New Beginning and *Muddy Paws* first published in Great Britain in 2008 by
Penguin Books Ltd., and in the United States in 2009 by Grosset & Dunlap.
This bind-up edition published in 2019 by Grosset & Dunlap, an imprint
of Penguin Random House LLC, New York. GROSSET & DUNLAP is a
trademark of Penguin Random House LLC.
Printed in the USA.

Visit us online at www.penguinrandomhouse.com.

The Library of Congress has cataloged the individual books under the
following Control Numbers: 2008040076, 2008040077.

ISBN 9780593222140   10 9 8 7 6 5 4 3 2 1

Contents

Magic Puppy

A New Beginning

SUE BENTLEY

To Cindy—first and best-beloved,
who was happy in a doll's pram.

A New Beginning

SUE BENTLEY

illustrated by Angela Swan

Prologue

Storm whimpered as he crawled into the cave. Behind the young silver-gray wolf, stars glimmered in the purple sky.

Suddenly, a piercing howl echoed in the night air.

"Shadow!" Storm gasped, trembling with fear.

The fierce lone wolf who had attacked Storm and the Moon-claw pack was close by. Storm knew he had to disguise himself, and quickly!

There was a dazzling gold flash and a fountain of golden sparks that lit up the back of the cave for a brief second. Where the wolf cub had just stood, there now crouched a tiny, sandy golden retriever puppy with floppy ears and twinkling midnight-blue eyes.

Storm's little puppy heart beat fast. In that split second of light, he had seen his mother, the she-wolf, lying crumpled against a rock.

"Mother?" he whined, plunging deeper into the cave.

"Storm?" Canista lifted her head to answer him in a velvety growl.

In the dim light Storm could see his mother's heaving sides and hear her rapid breathing. He felt a new surge of panic. "You are hurt! Did Shadow attack you, too?"

Canista nodded weakly. "His bite is poisoned. It drains my strength."

Storm's blue eyes flared with sorrow and anger. "Shadow has already killed my father and my three litter brothers. I will face Shadow and fight him!"

"Bravely said, my son. But now is not the time. You are the only cub left of our Moon-claw pack. Go to the other world. Use this puppy disguise to hide. Return when your magic is stronger. Then, together, we will fight Shadow." Canista's head flopped back tiredly as she finished speaking.

Storm bowed his head. He did not want to leave her, but he knew his mother was right.

The sound of mighty paws and a thunderous snarl echoed from the mouth of the cave.

"Go, Storm. Save yourself," Canista growled urgently.

Storm's sandy fur ignited with gold sparks. He whined softly as he felt the power building inside him. The golden light around him grew brighter. And brighter . . .

Chapter
ONE

Lily Benson felt a leap of excitement as her dad pulled up outside Greengates riding stables.

"Yay! I love Saturday afternoons. I get to spend hours and hours with ponies!" she cried, jumping out of the car.

Lily went around to the open window and bent down to kiss her dad's cheek.

Mr. Benson laughed. "Careful you

don't get pony-overload!"

"There's no such thing," Lily said. Her bedroom walls were covered with posters of ponies, and her bookcase was crammed with riding books and magazines.

"What a shame. I was hoping you might stop bugging your mom and me to buy you one!" her dad said.

He was only joking, but Lily felt a pang. She was desperate for a pony of her own. But her parents were worried about the hard work and amount of time it would take to care for it. Lily knew they were hoping she'd be satisfied with having free rides in exchange for helping out at Greengates.

"I'll never stop asking in a zillion years. Ponies rule, Dad!" she said.

"You've got a one-track mind, Lily

Benson. Have a good time. See you later,"
he called, steering away from the curb.

Lily sighed. She waved good-bye and
then went into the stable yard.

The main stable buildings were built
around two sides of a square. A large gate
at one end led to the grazing field. Just
beyond the field Lily could see the house
where Janie Green, who ran Greengates,
lived.

Janie was outside the tack room with
Treacle and Taffy, two of the smaller
ponies. Two young children in riding gear
stood waiting, ready to mount.

Janie looked up and smiled warmly
as Lily approached. She had a round
pretty face with twinkling brown eyes
and was always cheerful. "Hi, Lily. I hope
you're feeling energetic. We're fully

booked this afternoon."

"Hi, Janie," Lily said. She patted Taffy's neck and stroked Treacle's nose. "What do you want me to do first?"

"You could give Don a hand with the cleaning, if you don't mind. He's over at Bandit's stall," Janie said.

"Okay," Lily said happily. Bandit was her favorite pony. She was a sweet-natured palomino with a golden-tan coat and a pale mane and tail. Lily would have loved to own a pony just like her.

As Lily went off to find the stable boy she saw even more young riders arriving with their parents. It looked like it was going to be a hectic afternoon.

Lily said hello to Bandit for a few minutes, before spending the next hour or so forking up droppings, wheeling them over to the pile, and spreading fresh bedding.

Riders and ponies came and went. Lily lent a hand where it was needed. It was a hot day, and she was soon red-faced and sweaty.

"Why don't you take a break and go and get a drink?" Don suggested as she helped him fill the hay nets and water buckets. He was tall and wiry, with dark-red hair, freckles, and a thin face.

"Phew! I think I will," Lily said, pushing a strand of damp blond hair back from her forehead.

She went to the stable's kitchen and had a long, cold drink of orange juice.

As Lily was walking back past the grazing fields, she noticed some trash blowing around on the grass and went to pick it up.

"Thanks, Lily. You're doing a great job!" Janie Green called, pausing to rest the heavy saddle she was carrying on the fence.

"It makes me so mad when people

leave stuff behind. Don't they care that a plastic bag could kill a pony if it eats it?" Lily said indignantly.

"I don't think they give it a thought. Maybe they'd be more careful if they did—but not everyone's into horses."

Lily shrugged. "That's their loss, then!"

"I'm with you on that!" Janie said, smiling. "Have you persuaded your parents to buy you a pony yet?"

Lily made a face, thinking miserably of the earlier conversation with her dad.

"I take it that's a sore point," Janie said.

Lily nodded. "I still have to convince them that I can fit taking care of a pony around my schoolwork. Mom and Dad think it would be too much for me and I should wait until I'm older."

"They might be right, you know,"

Janie said gently. "Looking after a pony is a big commitment, and there are no days off."

Lily felt her spirits sink. She thought Janie would be on her side!

"Do you want to take Bandit out? We just got a cancellation, so she's free for a couple of hours," Janie said.

Lily brightened immediately at the thought of a longer free ride than usual. "Really? I can take her out by myself?" she asked delightedly.

Janie nodded. "You've ridden her plenty of times, and she's used to you. You can take her along the bridle paths, but don't go beyond the woods. Okay?"

Lily nodded, feeling proud that Janie trusted her. "Thanks, Janie! That's awesome!"

She dashed straight across to Bandit, who was already tacked up. "Hello, girl. We're going for a ride," she crooned, stroking the pony's nose.

Bandit gave a friendly neigh and nuzzled Lily's palm. Lily buckled on her riding hat before mounting the palomino pony and using her heels to nudge her forward.

They trotted out of Greengates and turned onto the bridle path that ran down the edge of a field. The path branched farther on and Lily took the way to the woods.

Other riders from the stables passed her on their way back.

As she and Bandit entered the shade of the trees, Lily's mind drifted into a wonderful daydream. It was easy to

imagine that Bandit was her own pony
and they were alone. The sound of other
riders was muffled, and she was screened
from them by the thick bushes. Sunlight
filtered through the leaves and speckled
everything with spots of light.

"I wish you were mine," Lily said
dreamily, leaning forward to pat Bandit's
satiny neck.

Suddenly Bandit stumbled on a tree root, and the reins were jerked right out of Lily's hands.

"Oh!" Lily pitched forward and fell right over the pony's neck. As the ground rushed up to meet her she closed her eyes, ready for the painful landing.

Chapter
TWO

The collision with the ground never
came.

With a dazzling golden flash and
a crackle of sparks, Lily found herself
jerking to a sudden halt. Her eyes flew
open in shock and she saw that she was
caught inside a huge glowing golden net,
in midair, half a foot above the ground!

Very slowly, Lily felt herself float down
and land gently on some leaves. With a
fizzing noise, the glowing net broke up
into golden sparks and then melted away
into the leaves.

Lily sat up, blinking confusedly. Her
first thought was for Bandit. She whipped
around and was relieved to see the pony
nibbling some grass in a small clearing a
few feet away.

"Your riding creature is fine. I hope
that you are not injured," said a strange
voice.

Lily stiffened. "W-who said that?"

A tiny puppy with sandy fur, floppy
ears, and huge midnight-blue eyes crawled
out from beneath a pile of leaves. "I did.
My name is Storm of the Moon-claw
pack. What are you? And what is the name

of your pack?" it woofed.

Lily's jaw dropped as she stared at the puppy in utter amazement. She felt like pinching herself to make sure she wasn't dreaming. But she saw that the puppy was looking at her quizzically as if waiting for her to respond.

"I'm a g-girl. A human . . . I'm L-Lily. Lily Benson," she found herself

stammering. "But I don't know what you mean about a pack."

"A human? I have heard of these." Storm's silky forehead wrinkled in a frown. Lily saw that he was beginning to tremble. "Can I trust you, Lily? I come from far away and I need your help."

Lily was still having difficulty taking this in, but she didn't want to frighten this amazing puppy away. He was absolutely gorgeous with the brightest midnight-blue eyes she had ever seen and big soft paws that looked too big for his body.

Very slowly she got up onto her knees and reached out her hand.

To Lily's delight, Storm edged closer and brushed her fingers with his damp little nose. His tail wagged nervously. Despite being so scared, the tiny puppy seemed to trust her.

"Why do you need my help?" she asked gently.

Storm's deep-blue eyes flashed with anger and sadness. "A lone wolf called Shadow attacked us. My father and brothers were killed and my mother is sick and in hiding. Shadow wants to lead the Moon-claw wolf pack, but the others will not follow him as long as I am alive."

"Wolf pack? But you're a pup—" Lily stopped as Storm held up a velvety sandy paw and began backing away.

There was another dazzling bright flash and a burst of gold sparks showered over Lily, crackling around her feet on the ground.

"Oh!" Lily rubbed her eyes, blinded for a second. When she could see again,

she saw that the tiny sandy puppy was gone. In its place now stood a majestic young wolf with thick silver-gray fur and glowing midnight-blue eyes.

"Storm?" Lily gasped, eyeing the wolf's large teeth and thick neck-ruff that glimmered with hundreds of gold sparks like tiny yellow diamonds.

"Yes, Lily, it is me," Storm said in a deep velvety growl.

Before Lily could get used to seeing

Storm as his magnificent real self, there
was a final gold flash and he appeared
once again as a cute sandy puppy.

"Wow! You really are a wolf. That's
an awesome disguise," she said, getting up
from her knees.

Storm began trembling again. "Not if
Shadow's magic finds me. Will you help
me hide?"

Lily's heart went out to the helpless
puppy. "Of course I will. You can live with
. . ." She trailed off as she remembered her
parents' rules about having no house pets.
They'd probably insist on taking Storm
to the pet care center. There must be
some way she could help the tiny puppy.
"Maybe I could smuggle you into my
house, but I don't see how I can hide you
for long," she said thoughtfully.

"Do not worry. I will use my magic so that only you will be able to see and hear me," Storm woofed.

"You can make yourself invisible? Wow!" Lily breathed. "No problem, then. You're coming home with me. Just let me catch Bandit. By the time we get back to Greengates, it'll be time for Dad to pick me up."

A few minutes later, as she cradled Storm in her lap on Bandit's back, a big smile spread across Lily's face. Never in her wildest dreams had she imagined having a magic puppy for a friend!

Chapter
THREE

"You should sleep in here in case Mom or Dad gets suspicious," Lily told Storm, spreading an old coat in the bottom of her closet. "But when no one's around, you can get on my bed."

Storm looked in the closet and then padded around her bedroom, sniffing everything and exploring. "This is a good place."

"Glad you like it!" Lily said, beaming at him. "Are you hungry?"

The tiny puppy barked eagerly.

"Okay. I'll go and raid the kitchen to see what I can find. I won't be long."

Lily dashed downstairs. Luckily her dad was in the garden cutting the lawn and her mom had just gone out to her yoga class. She found some leftover chicken in the fridge and quickly broke a piece off for Storm.

Back upstairs, she watched as Storm ate hungrily and then sat back licking his lips. "That was delicious. I like human food."

"I'll get you some dog food later," Lily said.

Storm nodded. "Good. We will go hunting together!"

"I couldn't do that!" Lily said, horrified. "Anyway, there's no need. The store at the end of the street sells dog food in cans. I'll buy some with my allowance," she told him.

Storm yawned, showing his sharp little teeth. "I think that I will rest now." Padding over to the closet, he curled up on the old coat with a contented sigh and promptly went to sleep.

Lily watched the tiny puppy's furry sides

rising and falling. Almost immediately his paws twitched as he started dreaming. *He must be exhausted from his long journey*, she thought.

Leaving Storm to sleep, Lily reached for a book of pony stories and stretched out on her bed to read.

The book was really good and she hardly noticed time passing. She was halfway through an exciting story about a pony being stolen, when something leaped onto her bed and launched itself on top of her.

Lily almost jumped out of her skin. "Storm! You scared me!" she said, laughing as she rolled over onto her back. "Did you have a good nap?"

"Yes, thank you. I feel safe here with you," Storm woofed happily. Plonking his

big soft paws on her book, he leaned up
and began licking her chin.

Lily wrapped her arms around his
plump little sandy body and gave him a
cuddle. After a couple of minutes, Storm
squirmed free and sprang onto the rug
with a surprisingly loud thud for a tiny
puppy.

"I would like to go outside now!"

"Okay," Lily said, getting up off the
bed. "Our garden's not very big, but
there's a field nearby. I'll take you for a
walk over there."

Storm gave an eager little bark and
followed her downstairs.

As they reached the hall, her dad
appeared at the living room door. He had
a frown on his face. "What was all that
thumping upstairs? It sounded like a herd
of elephants."

"Dad! I . . . er . . . thought you were
outside," Lily gasped in panic.

She quickly shifted around, trying
to stand in front of Storm, before she
suddenly remembered that he was
invisible. Then, realizing how strange
that must look, she began bending and
stretching her arms. "Whew! Whew!"

she puffed for added emphasis. "Just doing some exercise. I'm trying to get in shape. I was about to come and tell you that I'm going out for a jog around the field!"

Her dad raised his eyebrows as Lily did a jumping jack. "Well, I guess that's a good idea. Maybe I'll come with you. I could use some exercise, too."

"No!" Lily said hastily. "Someone . . .

um . . . from school might see me. I'll look like a real baby if I'm trailing around after you."

"Excuse me for trying to cramp your style," her dad joked. "What's brought this new fitness fad on?"

"I want to be ready for when I get my own pony! It's going to be hard work looking after it," Lily replied.

Her dad rolled his eyes. "I should have known what was at the bottom of this! Do you ever think of anything else besides ponies?"

"Nope! Well, actually, yes! But you wouldn't believe me if I told you!" Lily said, glancing at Storm, who was waiting by the front door. She jogged toward him before her dad could ask any more awkward questions. "See you later!"

Chapter
FOUR

As Lily put her school books into her bag on Monday morning, Storm sat watching her.

She smiled at him. "I love having you living here with me, but I have to go out for a few hours. Try not to get bored and chew my rug or anything, or Mom will freak!"

"I will not do anything like that,"

Storm yapped indignantly.

"Sorry. Sometimes I forget you're not an ordinary puppy," Lily said, bending down to pet his silky ears. "It's a shame there was only time for a quick walk around the field before breakfast. I'll take you out for a really long walk when I get back from school. Promise."

Storm looked up at her curiously. "What is school?"

"It's a place where kids go to learn. Teachers tell us stuff and give us homework to do, and we do projects and all kinds of things," Lily explained.

"School sounds interesting. I will come with you," Storm decided.

Lily grinned. "I wish you could, but pets aren't allowed . . ." She paused as she had a second thought. "Hey! Maybe you *can* come if you stay invisible! But you'd have to be really quiet and stay close to me. Mr. Poke, our class teacher, is very strict."

Storm's face brightened, and his little sandy tail started wagging with excitement. "I will make sure that no one will know I'm there—except you, Lily!"

"Cool! Let's go!" Lily put her backpack on the floor and opened it up.

"It might be best if you got inside. I have to cross some busy roads."

Storm jumped into her bag and settled next to her books and gym clothes. Lily put on her bag, said good-bye to her parents, and headed out of the front door.

"We'll probably meet Freema and Katy, my friends from class, on the way. I can't wait to see their faces when I tell them about you!" she said to Storm.

There was a scuffling noise from her bag. Storm popped his head out, his big dewy eyes looking into Lily's. "You cannot tell anyone my secret. Promise me, Lily," he woofed seriously.

Lily was disappointed. She had always wanted a pet to tell her friends about, especially a pony, but she had been really excited at the thought that she might be able to share her amazing magic puppy friend. She'd do anything if it would help keep Storm safe, though. "Okay, I promise. Cross my heart and hope to die," she said.

Storm nodded, satisfied.

As Lily and Storm reached the school gate, they saw Freema and Katy. There was another girl with them whom Lily hadn't seen before.

"Hi, Katy. Hi, Freema," Lily greeted her friends.

"Hi, Lily. This is my cousin, Adjoa," Freema explained. "She just moved here and is going to be in our class."

Adjoa was tall with shiny black hair, an oval face, and big brown eyes, just like Freema.

Lily smiled at her. "Welcome to our school, Adjoa."

"Thanks," Adjoa said shyly.

"Did you help out at Greengates this weekend?" Katy asked Lily as they walked into the school grounds.

Lily nodded. "It was great. I had an extra-long ride on Bandit. Janie let me take her up to the woods by myself."

"Cool!" Katy said.

"Do you like riding?" Adjoa asked Lily.

"It's my favorite thing in the whole world!" Lily replied. "How about you?"

"Adjoa loves ponies, too!" Freema said. She nudged her cousin. "Tell Lily about your pony."

Lily's eyes widened. "You've got your own pony? You're so lucky! What's its name?"

"Pixie. She's gorgeous and I love her to pieces," Adjoa said. "You can come over one night after school and meet her if you like."

"Thanks. I'd love to," Lily said, beaming.

In the classroom, Lily took her usual seat next to Katy. She put her bag on the floor, so that Storm could jump out.

Storm gave himself a shake and then trotted off to sniff around the room.

Mr. Poke took attendance. "And just before we begin," he said, looking up, "I'd like to welcome Adjoa Hardiker to the class."

Adjoa smiled shyly as everyone clapped, including Lily.

A few minutes later, Lily was leaning over to watch Storm. She smiled to herself as the tiny puppy weaved in and out of the desks, his sandy tail wagging.

A voice called out, but Lily was engrossed by Storm's cute antics.

"Lily Benson, can you stop daydreaming and take out your history book, please?" the teacher's sarcastic voice said. Mr. Poke had a bald head with a fuzzy rim of hair around his ears. He had a way of looking down his nose when he was annoyed.

Lily's head snapped up. "Sorry, sir."

"Looks like old Poker Face got out of bed on the wrong side—again," Katy commented. Adjoa and Freema, who sat nearby, giggled.

Lily turned around and grinned at them.

"Okay, class. I'd like you to begin work on your projects, please. Quietly, if possible!" Mr. Poke ordered.

They were doing the Tudors. Lily was making a collage of Queen Elizabeth I. "I think I'll do her lace ruffle today. I need to get some pieces of paper and stuff from the art cabinet," she said to Katy, who was bent over writing in her notebook.

"Can we have a little more work and a little less talking, Lily Benson?" Mr. Poke drawled.

"Yes, sir." Lily felt herself turning pink as she got up and went to the cabinet. *I wasn't even doing anything*, she thought.

Storm padded over to her. "Are you all right, Lily? You look hot," he woofed.

"I'm fine. Not like *some* people," Lily murmured, glancing back at the grumpy teacher.

She pulled the cabinet's handle, but it

seemed to have gotten stuck. Grasping it more firmly, she pulled again, but the door still wouldn't budge.

"I will help," Storm yapped eagerly.

Lily saw Mr. Poke coming over with a frown on his face. "Uh-oh, you'd better be quick, Storm. Looks like Poker Face is on the war path," she whispered.

Lily felt an odd, warm tingling down her spine as gold sparks ignited in Storm's sandy coat, and the tips of his ears and tail fizzed with power. Something strange was going to happen.

Raising one big sandy front paw, Storm sent a shower of bright golden sparks whooshing toward the cabinet. With a faint crackle they sank into the wood. For a moment nothing happened and Lily thought Storm's magic hadn't worked.

"Out of the way, Lily. Let me do it," Mr. Poke said irritably, reaching the cabinet—just as the doors sprang open.

An explosion of papers, brushes, pens, and paints shot out. Mr. Poke flew backward as if he'd been blown by a wind machine and landed on the floor on his backside.

Rustle! Papers floated down around him.

Splat! A plastic jar of glue hit Mr. Poke on the chest, bursting and spreading all over his gray sweater.

Thwack! Brushes, pens, and pencils fell on him, sticking firmly to the glue.

The teacher sat there blinking in shock.

The whole class erupted in laughter. Katy, Adjoa, and Freema were helpless.

Lily tried hard to bite back the
laughter bubbling up inside her.

"Who packed the cabinet like that?"
Mr. Poke roared, his face bright red as he
scrambled to his feet. "I have to go and
get cleaned up. Keep working, class. I'll be
right back." He stomped off toward the
bathroom, pens and pencils falling with a

clatter as he walked away.

"I am sorry, Lily. I think I used too much magic," Storm woofed in dismay.

Making sure that no one was looking, Lily quickly patted him. "You did just fine. It serves Mr. Poke right!"

She began putting everything back into the cabinet. Katy, Freema, and Adjoa helped her. By the time Mr. Poke reappeared wearing a hideous orange, yellow, and brown striped T-shirt, the mess was all cleared up.

The rest of the morning passed quickly, and at lunchtime Lily shared her cheese sandwiches and chips with Storm. When they finished, she took him for a run across the fields. The excited puppy ran around, chasing leaves in the wind and tiring himself out. He spent the rest of the afternoon napping under Lily's chair.

After school, with Storm back in her bag, Lily walked home with her friends.

She paused at the end of her street. "Did you mean it about me coming over to see Pixie?" she asked Adjoa.

Adjoa nodded. "Why don't you come over after school on Friday? We can both ride Pixie."

"That would be awesome!" Lily said. She jotted Adjoa's address and phone number in her notebook before heading home. "Bye. See you all tomorrow!" she called.

Katy, Freema, and Adjoa waved as they walked away.

Just inside her front garden, Lily put her bag down so that Storm could jump

out. "Adjoa's nice, isn't she?" she said to
him. "I can't wait to meet Pixie."

"Me too!" Storm nodded, his pink
tongue hanging in a doggy grin.

Lily felt a surge of affection for him.
She picked Storm up and petted his soft
sandy fur. "Having you at school today
was awesome! You really taught old Poker
Face a lesson. I hope that horrible Shadow
never finds you and then you can live with
me forever and come to school every day,"
she said.

"That is not possible, Lily," Storm told her, his small sandy face suddenly serious. "One day I must return to my own world to help heal my mother and fight Shadow."

Lily knew this was true, but she didn't want to believe it. She pushed all thoughts of Storm having to leave out of her mind and thought instead of the fun they would have on Friday with Adjoa and Pixie.

Chapter
FIVE

"Here you are, girl." Lily held a piece of carrot on the palm of her hand, so that Pixie could take it with her soft lips. Pixie was a chestnut pony with a white line down her nose and a friendly expression.

Lily turned to Adjoa as the pony crunched the treat. "Pixie is gorgeous!"

Adjoa smiled. "I know. I'm lucky to have her."

Pixie whinnied softly and swiveled
her ears.

"I think she agrees with you," Lily said.
They both laughed.

Adjoa opened the field gate and Lily
helped her saddle the pony, and then both
girls spent a couple of hours taking turns
riding her. Lily thought with a sigh how
wonderful it would be to have her own
pony and ride her every day.

Storm bounded alongside the pony
at first as Lily trotted around the field
on her, but his short legs soon got tired.
Lily couldn't lift him onto her lap with
Adjoa watching. "Are you okay? You're
not getting bored?" she leaned down to
whisper to him.

"I am fine. I will go and explore,"
Storm barked softly.

Lily watched him go frolicking off
toward the open-sided, wooden shelter at
the bottom of the field. She could see him
sniffing all the interesting smells in patches
of long grass on the way.

With Storm happily occupied, Lily
went back to enjoying her ride. Afterward
she helped Adjoa untack Pixie and then
rub her down before letting her run free.
The pony immediately threw herself onto
her back and rolled around. Storm ran
straight up to her barking happily.

"Oh no!" Lily gasped, only just
stopping herself from calling out to warn
Storm to be careful. If Pixie kicked, the
tiny puppy could get badly hurt by her
hooves.

"What's wrong?" Adjoa asked,
frowning.

"Er . . . nothing," Lily murmured, watching tensely as Pixie got to her feet again and shook herself. Her ears flattened as she looked down at the playful puppy, then she leaned down and gently nudged Storm's sandy fur. Storm yapped delightedly, wagging his tail.

Lily gave a big sigh of relief, which she quickly turned into a cough. She turned to Adjoa. "Sorry. I . . . um . . . thought I saw a rat in the straw in Pixie's shelter!"

Adjoa shrugged. "That's no big deal. The farmer's cats will catch it. Let's go in the house and get a drink." She opened

the field gate that led straight into her
back garden.

"Okay. I'll follow you in a sec. I think
I've got a stone in my boot." Bending
down so that she had her back to Adjoa,
Lily motioned to Storm.

Storm scampered straight over and
squeezed under the fence into the back
garden. He trotted at Lily's heel, panting
happily as they all walked toward the
house.

In the kitchen, Adjoa's mom was
getting cold drinks from the fridge. "I saw
you coming," she said, smiling. "You must
be Lily. It's nice to meet you. I'm glad
Adjoa's already made a new friend." Her
rows of tiny black braids were pinned up
into a bun. She wore gold hoop earrings,
jeans, and a pretty green top.

"Thanks for the drink, Mrs Hardiker,"
Lily said politely.

After their drinks, Lily and Storm
went up to Adjoa's room. "It's just like
mine!" Lily said delightedly, looking at all
the pony posters and books. Red and blue
ribbons that Adjoa had won for her riding
were pinned around her mirror.

"That was so much fun! Thanks,"
Lily said to Adjoa before she left for home.

"That's okay. You can come here
anytime," Adjoa said, smiling. "See you at
school on Monday!"

As she walked away with Storm,
Lily was thoughtful. "Adjoa's mom and
dad don't seem to have a problem with
their daughter taking care of a pony
and doing homework. But I don't think
I'll *ever* persuade mine to let me have one,"

she said to him with a sigh.

Storm barked in sympathy, wagging his tail. His thick sandy fur gleamed with tiny golden sparks. "Maybe I can help you," he woofed softly.

The following afternoon, Mrs. Benson dropped Lily and Storm off early at Greengates before she went to her yoga workshop. Lily had been silently thinking about what Storm had said; now she was bursting to ask him about it.

"Did you mean it, about helping me to get my own pony?" she asked as they walked across the stable yard.

Storm looked at her with alert midnight-blue eyes. "I did, Lily. I always keep my promises."

Lily waited, but Storm didn't say

anything more. Her imagination went into overdrive. "I bet you're going to use your magic to make a pony appear out of thin air, aren't you? Are you going to put Mom and Dad into a trance or something, so they let me keep it?" she asked excitedly.

Storm's furry brow dipped in a frown.
"No. That would not be the right thing to
do, Lily. I am afraid that you will have to
be patient," he woofed mysteriously. He
leaped forward and went off to explore
the yard, shedding a few tiny gold sparks,
which glinted in the bright sunlight
before dissolving.

Lily stared after Storm. She knew she
was going to have to do as he said, but it
was hard to be patient when you wanted
something so much.

It was time that she went to see what
jobs needed doing, but first Lily went
to visit Bandit. She had an apple in her
pocket for the pony.

But the palomino wasn't in her stable,
so Lily went to check the grazing field.
Bandit wasn't there either. As she was

walking back across the yard feeling
puzzled, Don came out of the tack room
holding a saddle.

"Is Bandit out on an early ride?" Lily
asked the stable boy.

"No. Bandit's already gone. Didn't
Janie tell you?" Don said.

"Gone? Gone where?" Lily asked.

"To her new home," Don explained.
"Bandit's quite old now, and Janie's been
thinking about retiring her for some time.
Someone came by during the week and
offered Bandit a new home on the spot.
Janie jumped at it. Bandit went to live in
a field with two goats and a donkey for
company."

"Oh, she'll really love that," Lily said,
trying hard not to feel sad. But she knew

she was really going to miss the gentle old pony.

Don's freckled face crinkled in a smile. "It's amazing that somewhere so perfect came right out of the blue, when Janie hadn't really started looking yet. Just like magic, really. Anyway, see you later." He went off to tack up a pony.

Storm came rushing across the yard, with a dusty nose from where he'd been searching around in some straw. He gave her a wide doggy grin and flopped down at her feet.

Lily looked down at him thoughtfully. "Did you have anything to do with finding Bandit a perfect new home, by any chance?"

Storm gave her a sideways look. He

twitched his nose. "I smell rabbits!" he yelped happily and shot off again toward the grazing field.

Lily stared after him. He was up to something, she was sure of it.

Chapter
SIX

It had been another busy afternoon at Greengates. Lily was hanging up a pile of newly cleaned bridles in the tack room.

Janie popped her head in the door. "Why don't you leave that and go have a ride? Tinka's still saddled up."

"Thanks, Janie!" Glancing over to where Storm was napping on top of the

brush box, Lily called to him. "Come on,
Storm."

Storm's head shot up immediately. He
jumped down and padded after Lily to
where Tinka was tied to the fence.

Lily buckled on her riding hat before
mounting the handsome bay pony. She
walked Tinka out of the yard and onto
the bridle path. This time she took the
fork leading to a field that the riding
school had permission to use. Storm ran
along beside her, his ears flapping as Lily
rode down a tractor path.

Lily had to concentrate very hard
when riding Tinka. The bay pony was
less experienced than dear old Bandit had
been. Lily dismounted and was opening
the field gate, when a wood pigeon
fluttered up out of a bush. Startled, Tinka
threw up her head and danced sideways.

"It's okay, girl." Lily spoke reassuringly,
petting Tinka's nose to calm her.

As Tinka backed up, Lily noticed a
ditch almost concealed in the long grass
by the hedge. Someone had dumped some
sharp hawthorn branches in it. Luckily,
Tinka had just missed it or she could have
been injured. Lily made a mental note to
tell Janie about the dangerous ditch when
she got back to Greengates.

Storm sat in her lap as Lily continued
her ride. But as she made her way back

an hour or so later he ran along beside
her again. She saw him run off into the
field and start jumping around, barking
at butterflies and sticking his nose in
molehills. By the time Lily got back to the
field gate and dismounted again, Storm
was behind her.

Lily led Tinka through and was closing
the gate, when she spotted a familiar pony
and rider coming toward her along the
edge of the field. "Look, Storm! It's Adjoa
on Pixie!" she cried delightedly.

A moist brown nose and then two
sandy ears appeared as Storm squeezed
through a small gap in the hedge. He gave
an excited bark and leaped toward the
long grass.

Lily realized that he was heading
straight for the concealed ditch. "Storm!

Look out!" she cried. But the puppy was
so set on reaching his friend Pixie that he
didn't hear her.

Lily threw herself forward. She missed
Storm, but just managed to push him
sideways as she lost her balance and slid
into the ditch.

"Ow!" she gasped with pain as her

ankle twisted and sharp thorns dug into
her leg.

Storm looked down at her in dismay.
"You saved me, Lily. But you are hurt. I
will help you," he whined.

"I . . . I think I'm okay," Lily said
shakily, biting back tears at the sharp ache
in her leg. Her riding pants were torn and
smeared with grass stains.

Time seemed to stand still. Lily felt
a familiar warm tingling down her back
as vivid gold sparks ignited in Storm's
fur. His tail stiffened and crackled with
power. Raising a velvety front paw Storm
sent a whoosh of sparks fizzing toward
Lily's injured leg. For a second the pain
increased and then it drained away just as
if someone had poured it down a drain.

When the bright sparks faded,

Lily saw that her riding pants were clean and fixed, too. "Thanks, Storm," she whispered.

"You are welcome," Storm woofed as the final gold sparks faded from his thick sandy fur.

Lily quickly climbed out of the ditch. She stood up as Adjoa pulled Pixie to a halt a couple of feet away. "Watch out for this ditch. You can hardly see it. I . . . er . . . nearly just slipped right into . . . ," she blustered. Lily racked her brain for an explanation that didn't involve Storm, but Adjoa wasn't listening.

Her new friend's eyes were red and puffy. It was obvious that Adjoa had been crying. Lily felt sad for her friend. What could be wrong?

Lily held Tinka by her reins and listened with growing dismay to what Adjoa had to say.

"The farmer who we rent Pixie's field from is selling it and we can't find another field nearby. Mom and Dad say it would cost too much to put her into stables where she'd be cared for, and so we might have to sell her," Adjoa said tearfully.

"Oh no! That's terrible," Lily exclaimed, putting one arm around her friend.

She knew it was expensive to have a

pony looked after by a stable. But it was
awful to think of Adjoa losing her beloved
pony.

Beside her Pixie gave a friendly blow
and dipped her head to nuzzle Storm
gently. The tiny puppy was lying on his
back in the grass with all four legs in the
air, showing his fat pale tummy. For once,
Lily felt too upset for Adjoa to smile at his
playful antics.

An idea came to her. She was going to
talk to her parents.

Chapter
SEVEN

"I'm sorry, Lily. But my answer has to be the same," Mrs. Benson said.

They were all sitting in the kitchen on Saturday evening. Storm was lying down next to Lily's chair, invisible to everyone except her, as usual. Lily had just finished explaining about Pixie in the hope that her parents might be willing to buy the pony.

"I agree with your mom," Mr. Benson said. "Looking after a pony is a big responsibility. We're just not sure this is the right time for you to take that on."

"But it is, Dad! I'd be the best pony owner ever!" Lily said in her best pleading voice. "And if we bought Pixie, Adjoa could still see her whenever she wanted."

Her dad smiled and reached out to ruffle her hair. "I'm sorry, honey. I feel bad for Adjoa, too, but the subject's closed."

"That's what I thought you'd say," Lily said, sighing heavily.

All that evening and throughout Sunday, Adjoa and Pixie were on Lily's mind. On Monday, when she and Storm walked to school, they met up with Katy and Freema, but Adjoa wasn't with them.

"Where's Adjoa?" Lily asked.

"She's not coming in today. My aunt says she's got an upset tummy," Freema explained.

"I know *why* Adjoa's tummy is upset. It's because she's so worried about what's going to happen to Pixie," Lily said sadly.

Freema and Katy nodded.

When they reached the coatroom, Lily hung back and let her friends go into school ahead of her. "I wish I could think of a way to help Adjoa keep Pixie," she whispered to Storm. "But I've already tried Mom and Dad. I don't know what else I can do."

Storm whined softly in sympathy and then his big midnight-blue eyes lit up. "You could talk to the lady who runs the riding stables," he suggested.

"Janie? I can't see what good that would do," Lily said, frowning.

Storm barked encouragingly, wagging
his tail and dancing around her feet in
circles. Lily smiled. "Well, okay then, if
you're that sure it'll help. We'll stop over
there tonight after school. Uh-oh! Watch
out! Mr. Poke just came in. We'd better go
into class!" she hissed out of the side of
her mouth.

Back home after school, Lily quickly
changed into her jeans and T-shirt, before
running downstairs. She found her mom
in the kitchen. "Could you give me a ride
over to Greengates, please?" she asked.

Her mom looked surprised. "Don't
you get enough of that place on the
weekends? Why do you want to go over
there now?"

Lily thought quickly. "Tinka was sick

on Saturday. I wanted to check and see if she's any better," she lied.

Mrs. Benson smiled. "That's nice of you. You're a sweet person, Lily Benson."

Lily blushed, feeling a little guilty. But there was no way she could tell her mom that it was Storm's suggestion to go and talk to Janie. Anyway, it was true that she was always happy to see Tinka and all the other ponies. "So can I have a ride?" she asked.

Her mom nodded. "We'll go now. I have to go to the supermarket, so I can drop you off at Greengates and then pick you up on my way back."

Lily sat in the back of the car, with Storm on her lap as they drove there. She got out of the car at Greengates's main entrance. "Thanks for the ride, Mom.

I'll see you later."

As soon as her mom had driven away, Lily went into the yard. Storm trotted purposefully at her heels, invisible as usual.

She could see Janie sitting at her computer through the office window.

Lily paused, feeling uncertain. "Well, here I am. But I'm still not sure why! What am I supposed to say to her?" she whispered to Storm.

The puppy's luminous midnight-blue eyes looked even brighter than usual. "I think you should tell Janie about how Pixie needs a home," he woofed.

Lily frowned. "But there's no point. Greengates isn't a stable. It's a riding school. And anyway, Janie doesn't have room for any extra ponies. All the loose boxes are full."

Storm pricked his ears. "Not all of them."

Lily blinked as she realized what Storm was hinting at. "You're right! Bandit's not here anymore."

Storm nodded, looking very pleased with himself.

Before Lily could ask him anything else, Janie came out into the yard. "Lily? This is a nice surprise. What can I do for you?" she said.

"I . . . um . . ." Lily bit her lip, feeling

herself blushing as she struggled to find
the right words to say. Now that she was
here, her mind seemed to have gone
completely blank.

Chapter
EIGHT

Storm gave a gentle woof, and as Lily looked down into his sparkling midnight-blue eyes, she felt herself starting to calm down.

Lily took a deep breath, and suddenly it all came pouring out. "I . . . um . . . wanted to ask you something. I've got a friend named Adjoa who's got a pony named Pixie. She's very sweet-natured, but

the farmer who owns her field is selling it.
And I thought, well, I was hoping—"

Janie smiled. "Whoa! Slow down a bit.
Let's go into my office, Lily. I could use a
break from working on my accounts. We'll
have a cold drink and you can tell me all
about it."

A few minutes later, Lily sat sipping
her apple juice as Janie tapped her fingers
on the desk thoughtfully.

"So what you're really asking is for
me to put Pixie into the stable?" she said
to Lily.

Lily nodded, feeling encouraged by
Janie's calmness and willingness to listen.
Everything seemed to have slotted into
place and become clear in her mind. Now
Lily knew exactly what to say.

"What about if Pixie lives here

and works as one of the riding school
ponies? Adjoa would have to agree, but
I think she'd do anything if it meant she
could keep Pixie. She'd still own her,
so she'd help look after her and pay for
Pixie's food and bedding and stuff. But it
probably wouldn't cost anywhere near as
much as a normal stable."

"You seem to have this all worked
out," Janie said.

"I do!" Lily said firmly.

"Hmm. It could work. We've had arrangements like this in the past and we are a pony short now that Bandit's gone. But I'd have to try Pixie out before I decided that she was right for Greengates. She'd have to be gentle, friendly, and dependable."

"Oh, she is! She's perfect. Should I ask Adjoa's parents to call you and set up a meeting?" Lily asked eagerly.

Janie nodded, smiling. "Yes. You're one determined young lady, Lily Benson."

"That's what my dad says!" Lily beamed at Janie as she got up. "Thanks so much, Janie. Is it okay if I go and see Tinka and the other ponies? I have just enough time before Mom picks me up."

"Of course it is. I'll leave you to it. I'd better get back to these accounts."

Lily and Storm spent twenty minutes with the ponies before going back to the riding stable's entrance. Mrs. Benson had just arrived and was waiting to pick her up.

On the way home in the back of the car, Lily stroked Storm's floppy sandy ears.

"You had this all worked out, didn't you?" she said softly.

Storm nodded. "But I could not have done it all by myself. It was you who spoke to Janie. You did it, Lily."

Lily felt a warm glow of pride. It felt good to have helped her friend. "I can't wait to tell Adjoa all about it. I'm going to call her as soon as I get home."

The moment her mom pulled into the driveway, Lily shot out of the car and dashed toward the house.

"Er, excuse me, young lady! I could use some help with the groceries," her mom called after her.

"Sorry," Lily said sheepishly.

She rushed back, grabbed some bags, and dumped them on the kitchen table.

As she was coming out of the kitchen, the phone rang.

It was Adjoa's mom. "Hello, Lily. Is Adjoa with you? Can I have a word with her, please?" she asked.

"She isn't here," Lily replied, puzzled.

"Oh my, I was hoping she'd ridden Pixie over to see you," Mrs. Hardiker said, sounding worried. "Could I talk to your mom?"

Lily passed the phone over. "It's Adjoa's mom."

Lily waited impatiently while the two moms spoke. "What's going on?" she asked as her mom hung up the phone.

"Adjoa left a note saying she couldn't handle giving up Pixie, and some of her clothes are missing. Mrs. Hardiker was hoping she'd come over here. But it's beginning to look like Adjoa has run away with Pixie."

"Oh no!" Lily gasped.

Chapter
NINE

"It'll be dark soon. Adjoa must be so
scared. We have to find her and tell her
the news about Greengates!" Lily said to
Storm as soon as they were alone in her
bedroom.

Storm nodded. "I will take us to
Adjoa's house and see if I can pick up a
fresh trail."

Lily felt a familiar warm tingling down

her back as gold sparks crackled in Storm's
sandy fur and a fountain of golden glitter
streamed out of his tail. There was a bright
flash and a whooshing sensation, and
suddenly Lily found herself standing with
Storm outside Pixie's field at the back of
Adjoa's house.

Storm sniffed around, picking up
Pixie's scent. Moments later, he stiffened.
Lily saw that his moist brown nose was
glowing like a gold nugget. "This way!" he
barked, setting off at a run.

Lily followed Storm away from the
field and through the streets. They hurried
along the main road and then toward the
edge of town. The street lights had already
come on. Overhead the first stars had
begun twinkling in the sky.

Lily grew hot and sweaty as she and

Storm followed Pixie's trail, but she
wasn't tired. Gold sparks flashed past her
as Storm's magic made them travel in
double-quick time. Gradually Lily realized
where they were heading.

"Greengates is just over there. Adjoa
must have taken the bridle path. I bet she's
planning to hide in the woods overnight.
She'll probably take the shortcut across the
fields," she told Storm.

A few minutes later, Storm barked and
wagged his tail. "Over there!"

In the twilight, Lily could just make
out the figure of a pony and rider against
the shadowy bushes. The moon came out
from behind a cloud and Lily could see
more clearly. "It's them!" she cried.

Lily saw that Pixie was trotting toward
the familiar field gate. "That ditch! Adjoa's

heading straight for it. Those prickly
branches have been cleared away since I
told Janie about it, but a pony could still
break her leg if she stumbles into it. I bet
she's too upset to remember it's there, and
Pixie won't see it in the dark!"

Storm's midnight-blue eyes flashed.
Another rainbow of sparks shot out ahead
of him and he leaped forward into the
stream of light. Lily felt herself shooting

through the air beside him. She and Storm
landed a few feet in front of Adjoa and
Pixie.

Lily walked forward, holding up her
arms. "It's me, Lily! Adjoa, stop!"

Adjoa reined Pixie in. The pony's ears
swiveled and her head came up, but she
halted calmly a few paces away from the
ditch.

"Lily! What are you doing here? How
did you find me?" Adjoa cried.

"Don't worry about that now," Lily
said. "That ditch I fell into the other day
is right in front of you. Pixie could have
stumbled into it. Come over here. I have
to tell you something."

Adjoa urged Pixie over to one side,
but she didn't dismount. She looked
shaken, but determined. "Thanks for

reminding me about that ditch. But if you're going to try and persuade me to go back home, don't bother!" Adjoa said, looking down at Lily.

"Adjoa, listen! I've got some great news," Lily said quickly before her friend could decide to ride away. "I talked with Janie at Greengates. She's willing to take Pixie into her stable on the condition that you let her be used for the riding school."

"Really?" Adjoa looked stunned, but her hands loosened on the reins. Her shoulders relaxed as she thought about it. "I wouldn't mind little kids riding Pixie, and she'd enjoy the extra exercise. Dad said she was getting a bit fat anyway. But even with Janie using Pixie for rides, it's still going to cost a lot to keep her stabled at Greengates. I still don't know if Mom

and Dad will agree."

Lily's face fell. She hadn't thought of this. It seemed as if there was a flaw in her awesome plan.

Storm jumped up with his paws on Lily's leg and woofed for attention. Lily looked down at him. "You could ask your mom and dad to help," he suggested in a soft bark.

It was a few seconds before Storm's words sank in. "That's it!" she burst out, her eyes widening.

"What is?" Adjoa said, puzzled.

"I just had a brilliant idea. Come on, Adjoa. We're going back to talk to my parents!" She quickly outlined her plan.

A look of hope came over Adjoa's face. "Do you think they'll agree?"

"They have to. It's Pixie's last chance," Lily said determinedly, turning on her heel, confident that Adjoa would now follow her on Pixie. At her side, Storm gave an encouraging yelp.

Chapter
TEN

Later that evening, Lily sat at the kitchen table eating a pizza with her mom and dad. Storm was curled up under the table.

"You did a great job persuading Adjoa to come home," her dad said. "Her parents were almost out of their minds with worry. They've been on the phone saying how great you are. Good work, sweetie."

Lily felt herself blushing. "Anyone would have done the same."

"I'm not sure that's true," her mom said, patting her hand. "What I still can't figure out is how you found her so quickly and got up to the field near Greengates in record time."

"It must be all the exercise I've been doing. Mmm. This pizza's delish!" Lily said, quickly changing the subject. She slipped a small piece under the table for Storm to munch. "Mo-om? Da-ad?" she said in a persuading voice. "I've . . . um . . . got something to ask you."

Her parents exchanged glances. "I hope this isn't about having your own pony again!" Mrs. Benson said.

"Of course it's not," Lily said brightly.

"Thank goodness for that!" her dad said.

Lily paused for effect. "It's about me having half a pony!"

Mr. Benson frowned. "Run that by me again."

Lily grinned. "What I really mean is *sharing* a pony!" She explained about Janie agreeing to take Pixie into the stable and being a riding school pony. "But it's still going to be very expensive, so Adjoa's parents might decide to sell Pixie anyway. But they won't if we help with the costs.

And then I'd be sort of sharing a pony with Adjoa. I'd be able to groom Pixie and ride her sometimes. What do you think?"

"I think Pixie's going to be one busy pony!" her dad said, smiling. "But it's an interesting idea."

Lily held her breath and had all her fingers and toes crossed. At least her dad hadn't said no right away like he usually did.

"I know you, Lily. You'll want to be up at Greengates every night, looking after Pixie and grooming her," said Mrs. Benson. "I'm still worried that your schoolwork could suffer."

"I know I might want to do that, but I won't, because I'll know that I have to take turns with Adjoa," Lily said honestly. "I'll just be so happy to be able to ride

Pixie sometimes—and pretend she's all mine until I get a pony of my own one day!"

Her mom and dad exchanged glances.

"Well, when you put it like that, it sounds like a fair arrangement," her mom said.

"And it's the only way Lily's ever going to give us any peace! So the answer's yes," her dad added.

"Yay!" Lily flung herself at her parents and gave them both huge hugs and then did a little dance around the table. "I can't wait to tell Adjoa!"

Storm ran out from under the table and jumped up and down, barking excitedly. Lily grinned and just barely managed to stop herself from bending down and picking him up.

Later that night, Lily closed her
bedroom curtains, getting ready for bed.
Outside in the street she saw a
couple of people taking their dogs for a

walk. She jumped into bed and snuggled up under the blankets with Storm.

"Thanks so much for everything, Storm. You kept your promise about helping me get a pony, even though things turned out differently than how I imagined! You're the most awesome friend ever. We're going to have an amazing summer with Pixie and Adjoa!"

Storm tucked his head under her chin. "I am glad I was able to help."

Suddenly Lily heard howling and growling from outside in the street. She jumped back out of bed and peered through the bedroom curtains. The two dog walkers were struggling to control their dogs, which were pulling at their leashes and looking up at her bedroom. In the light of the streetlamps, the dogs' eyes looked pale and were glowing.

"That's weird . . ." Lily said, turning to Storm.

The tiny puppy was hiding in the bed. She could see him trembling with fright.

Frowning, Lily glanced outside again and saw the dogs suddenly calm down. After a moment, their confused owners walked on until they were out of sight.

Lily came back to Storm. As she went to pet him she realized that he was still shaking all over. "What's wrong? Are you sick?" she asked worriedly.

Storm shook his head. His ears were laid back and his tail was tucked beneath him. "I sense that Shadow is close. I think he used his magic, so that the dogs outside would attack me."

Lily looked at her friend in dismay. "Is that what he'll do if he finds you?"

Storm nodded, his eyes as dull as blue stones. "All the dogs around here will be looking for me now. I will use my magic to mask my scent. It may give me a little more time."

Lily kissed the top of his sandy head, breathing in his sweet puppy smell, and lay awake, hoping that Storm would be safe. She didn't think she could bear it if she never saw him again.

Chapter
ELEVEN

Lily woke up with a start the next morning. To her relief, Storm was curled up asleep next to her.

He seemed more like his normal self, but his sparkling midnight-blue eyes were still concerned. "I will stay here and hide. I want to be sure that Shadow cannot sense where I am," he barked.

Lily felt reluctant to leave him, but she

had promised to meet Adjoa at Greengates
and help settle Pixie into her new home.

"I'll see you later," she said, bending
down to kiss the top of Storm's warm
silky head.

Storm curled himself into a tight ball
and didn't answer.

"Whoa, there, girl!" Janie Green said
gently.

Lily and Adjoa stood watching as
Janie backed Pixie out of the horse trailer,
hitched to her Land Rover. "That's it.
Good. Come on."

Pixie slowly moved backward, step
by step. Finally she stood in the stable
yard, her legs trembling slightly and her
chestnut coat twitching.

"Good girl," Adjoa said gently, going

over to pet Pixie's nose. "She's feeling nervous. She's been used to living in a field by herself."

"It's only natural for her to feel unsettled," Janie said understandingly.

"She's used to you, so why don't you and
Lily lead her around for a little before you
take her into the loose box? Call me if
you have any problems. Okay?"

"Okay. Thanks." Adjoa looked over at
Lily as Janie went to park her Land Rover.
"Janie's really nice, isn't she?"

Lily smiled and nodded. "There are
lots of strange new smells here. Why don't
you walk Pixie past the grazing field a few
times? It might calm her if she smells fresh
grass like in her field," she suggested to
Adjoa.

"That's a good idea."

For the next twenty minutes Adjoa led
Pixie around the yard, talking gently to
her the entire time.

Lily watched, trying not to think
about Storm and whether he was still safe.

But her worries about her tiny puppy
friend kept pushing into her mind.

Pixie gradually seemed to relax.
Finally, Adjoa felt confident enough to
lead her to Bandit's old loose box, which
was going to be her new home. Earlier,
Lily had covered it with a deep layer
of clean bedding. There was a hay net
hanging up and clean water in a bucket.

Lily opened the door wide.

Adjoa went to lead Pixie inside. But
Pixie rolled her eyes and stood still. "Come
on. It's lovely in there. There's space for
you to turn around and lie down if you
want to," she encouraged.

Pixie shifted nervously and rolled her
eyes. "She's just not comfortable with
going indoors," Adjoa said.

"I'll get some carrots from the feed

store. That might tempt her to go in," Lily said.

"Good idea," Adjoa said gratefully.

Lily returned quickly. But the carrots didn't work either.

"What if we can't get Pixie to go in at all?" Adjoa said worriedly. "Janie might change her mind about her. She won't want an awkward pony at the riding school."

"That's not going to happen. Pixie's just scared. She's going to be fine," Lily said reassuringly, but she was starting to get concerned.

If only Storm was here. He'd calm Pixie down. But Storm had to fight his own battle, hiding from his enemy—the fierce wolf Shadow.

"I think I'd better go and get Janie or

Don, after all," Lily decided reluctantly after another fifteen minutes of leading Pixie around and a second failed attempt at getting her to go into her box.

"Okay, then." Adjoa was almost in tears.

Just then Lily heard a rustling sound from inside the loose box. A spurt of bright golden sparks shot up out of the straw and a cute sandy face appeared.

"Storm!" Lily exclaimed delightedly and then realized that Adjoa was giving her a strange look. "I mean . . . it looks like rain or something. I think we should try Pixie one more time before we go and get help."

Adjoa looked doubtful, but she nodded.

Pixie stretched out her neck and blew

a warm breath toward Storm. Storm
barked encouragingly and wagged his tail.

Pixie lifted one front leg. She took a
step forward and then another one. She
went inside and Adjoa closed the door
after her. "Phew! At last! I thought she'd
never go in," she said, relieved.

"She'll be fine now. Why don't you go
and tell Janie?" Lily suggested.

Just as Adjoa disappeared into the
office, Storm whined in terror. He leaped
over the stable door into the yard, trailing
a bright comet's tail of golden sparks, and

streaked toward the tack room.

Lily whipped around and saw two small dogs coming through the main gates. They raised their heads, and she saw their abnormally long teeth and fierce pale wolf eyes. Her heart skipped a beat. They were here for Storm!

She dashed across the yard and rushed into the empty tack room.

There was a bright golden flash. Lily blinked hard as her vision cleared. Storm stood there as his magnificent real self. The majestic young wolf's dazzling silver-gray fur gleamed, and his midnight-blue eyes glowed like sapphires. A she-wolf with a gentle tired face stood next to Storm.

And then Lily knew that this time Storm was leaving for good.

"Our enemies are very close. We must

go!" Storm's mother rumbled.

Storm raised a large silver paw in
farewell. "You have been a good friend.
Be of good heart, Lily," he said in a deep
velvety growl.

Lily's throat closed with tears and
there was an ache in her chest. She was

going to miss Storm terribly. "Good-bye, Storm. Take care. I'll never forget you," she whispered hoarsely.

There was a final bright flash and a crackle of gold sparks that sprinkled down around her like warm rain. Storm and his mother faded and then disappeared. The dogs ran into the tack room. Lily saw their teeth and eyes instantly return to normal before they turned and slunk away.

Lily blinked away tears as she went slowly back out into the yard. At least she'd had a chance to say good-bye to Storm. She knew she'd never forget the wonderful adventure she'd shared with the magic puppy.

Although she could never tell another person about Storm, there was someone else who was going to miss the tiny puppy and with whom she could share all her thoughts. Pixie!

As Lily went toward Pixie's stall and saw Adjoa coming out of Janie's office, she smiled at the thought of all the adventures they were going to have with their very own pony!

Magic Puppy

Muddy Paws

SUE BENTLEY

To Petra—gentle sheepdog friend
and a loyal companion.

Magic Puppy

Muddy Paws

SUE BENTLEY

illustrated by Angela Swan

Prologue

Storm paused to drink the clear water that flowed swiftly between two banks of ice. It felt good to be back in his home world.

But the young silver-gray wolf's happiness lasted for only a moment as he thought of his mother, Canista, wounded and in hiding.

Suddenly a terrifying howl echoed in

the icy wind.

"Shadow!" Storm gasped, realizing that the fierce lone wolf was close.

Storm used his magic to transform himself quickly so he would be hidden from Shadow. There was a bright flash and a dazzling shower of golden sparks. Where Storm had been standing there now crouched a tiny fluffy black-and-white Border collie puppy with midnight-blue eyes.

Storm trembled, hoping that his puppy disguise would protect him from the evil Shadow. Keeping his little belly low to the ground, Storm crept into a clump of snow-covered bushes.

A dark shape pushed through the bushes, loosening a cloud of snow, and Storm's tiny heart missed a beat. Shadow had found him!

But instead of the lone wolf's dark-gray muzzle and pitiless black eyes, Storm saw a familiar silver-gray face with bright golden eyes.

"Mother!" he yapped with relief.

"I am glad you are safe and well, my son, but you have returned at a dangerous time," Canista said in a warm velvety growl. She nuzzled the disguised cub's black-and-white face, but then gave a sharp wince of pain.

"Shadow's poisonous bite sapped your strength!" Storm blew out a gentle stream of tiny gold sparks, which sank into Canista's injured leg and disappeared.

"Thank you, Storm. The pain is easing. But there's no time right now for you to help me recover all my powers. You must

go—Shadow is very close," Canista
rumbled softly.

Sadness rippled through Storm's tiny
puppy body as he thought of his dead
father and litter brothers and the once
proud Moon-claw wolf pack, now
broken up. His midnight-blue eyes
flashed with anger. "One day I will stand
beside you and face Shadow!"

Canista nodded proudly. "But until
then, you must hide in the other world.
Use this puppy disguise and return when
your magic is stronger."

Another fierce howl split the air. "I
know you are close, Storm! Come out
and let us finish this!" Shadow cried in
an icy growl.

"Go now, Storm! Save yourself!"
Canista urged.

Bright gold sparks ignited in the tiny black-and-white puppy's fur. Storm whined softly as he felt the power building inside him. Bright golden light surrounded him. And grew brighter . . .

Chapter
ONE

Beth Hollis woke up with a start and lay looking up at the unfamiliar white ceiling with its low black beams. Rain pattered against the window, and she could hear animal noises and voices outside.

Gradually Beth recognized the attic bedroom in the Tail End Farm owned by her aunt and uncle. She was staying here while her parents were away.

The room was still dark, and a gust of
wind sent more rain drumming against
the window. Beth pulled the blanket over
her head and snuggled back under the
downy warmth.

Suddenly the bedroom door swung
open. Beth heard muffled footsteps

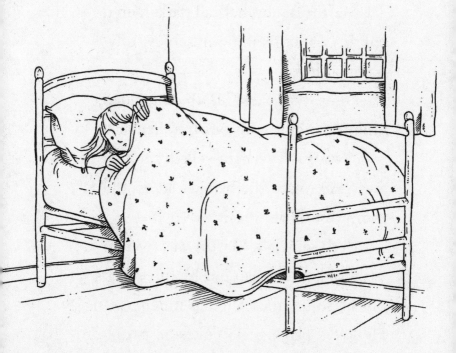

approaching the bed and then she felt a
rush of cool air as the blanket was pulled
aside.

"Rise and shine!" cried a voice.
"Mornings start early on a farm!"

"Hey!" Beth complained, sitting
straight up.

Martin Badby, her tall dark-haired
cousin, stood grinning mischievously
down at her.

"Give that back!" Beth demanded,
lunging at him with outstretched arms.

"No way!" Martin yelled, backing
away. He tossed the blanket across the
room out of her reach.

Beth scowled. Martin was twelve
years old, older than her by three years,
but he sometimes acted as if he were six.
He loved playing silly jokes on people,

especially his younger cousin.

"That was a really mean thing to do!" she yelled.

"Yeah? So sue me!" Martin said cheerfully. "Are you coming downstairs, or what?"

Beth sat in the middle of her bed and crossed her arms. "No, I am not! Auntie Em said I didn't have to get up early on my first day here!"

"That's only 'cause you were sulking last night. I heard you talking to your mom and dad before they left. 'Poor me. It's *so* awful that I have to stay at boring Tail End,'" he mimicked in a silly whiny little voice.

"I don't talk like that!" Beth said, feeling her cheeks turn red. "Anyway, how would you like it if you got dumped on relatives while your parents flew to England for two weeks?"

Martin rolled his eyes. "They're not going anywhere fun, are they? It's just a boring business trip."

"I still wanted to go with them," Beth murmured. She'd never been away from her parents, except for the occasional sleepover at a friend's house, and she was really going to miss them.

"Talk about selfish. I guess you didn't even think about me?" Martin grumbled.

Beth frowned, puzzled. "What about you?"

"Well, *I* have to put up with *you*, don't I? Mom and Dad have practically ordered me to look after you. Just what I wanted, my stupid spoiled cousin following me around—not!"

"Thanks a lot! I'll try not to get in your way!" Beth cried indignantly. She flung herself off the bed and stomped over to the closet. "Can you leave now, please? I want to get dressed."

"I thought you weren't getting up?" Martin teased.

"I changed my mind. Spoiled cousins do that a lot, you know!" Beth said spiritedly.

"Whatever!" Martin went out and closed the bedroom door behind him.

Beth made a face at the closed door. She'd forgotten how annoying her cousin could be, and now it seemed that he wasn't happy having her here at all. Her spirits sank even further as she thought of the two weeks stretching endlessly ahead of her.

"Morning, Beth. You're up early. Did you sleep well?" Emily Badby called from the yard as Beth stood in the open doorway of the back porch.

"Fine, thanks," Beth replied. *No thanks to Martin*, she thought.

Her aunt held a bucket of vegetables. "Goats love fresh food. It gets them in a good mood for milking. Do you want to come and watch?"

"Okay," Beth said, shrugging. She wasn't that interested in goats, but there was still so much time before breakfast and nothing else to do.

She borrowed a pair of boots and followed her aunt into the barn. A sweet musty smell of goats, dung, and warm hay greeted her. "Phew!" Beth said as she wrinkled her nose.

Emily Badby laughed. "It's a healthy farm smell. You'll get used to it."

Beth wasn't sure she wanted to. She went to look at the brown-and-white goats in their pens, down one side of the barn. "They all look a little annoyed. What kind are they?" she asked.

"Anglo-Nubians. It's their long noses and floppy ears that give them that expression," Emily explained, selecting a goat and leading it to a small wooden platform. The goat leaped up nimbly, and soon Beth was watching the creamy milk foaming into a clean bucket. "I sell milk, yogurt, and cheese in the local stores," Emily said. "My dairy's next door. You can have a look around sometime, but ask me first. I have strict rules about hygiene."

Beth nodded.

When her aunt finished milking, she poured the milk through a filter into a metal churn. "I'll just take this to the dairy and then get started on breakfast."

A loud braying noise came from the back of the barn. "Oh! What's that?" Beth looked around in surprise.

Her aunt laughed. "That's Darcy, my new billy goat. He's only been here for a week or so, but he's always complaining because he isn't getting any attention."

"Can I go and say hello to him?" Beth asked.

"Yes, of course, but be—" The rest of her aunt's reply was drowned out by a loud irritable voice in the doorway.

"There you are!" Martin cried, standing aside as his mom left. "What are you hiding in here for?"

"I wasn't hiding! Auntie Em said I could watch her milking," Beth said.

Martin flicked back a strand of wet dark hair. "Anyway, Dad said I had to ask you if you wanted to come with me to take Ella for a walk." Ella was the family's old black-and-white Welsh Border collie.

"No thanks," Beth said, feeling annoyed that he'd only asked her because his dad had made him. Turning on her heel, she went toward the back of the barn. "I'm going to look at Darcy."

"Hang on! I'll come with you. Ella won't mind waiting for her walk. I have to drag her out half the time anyway. Since Dad retired her from farm work, she's really stiffened up," Martin said.

Darcy's pen was behind some straw bales. He was a handsome dark-brown goat with a white neck. "It looks like he's wearing a cute white collar!" Beth exclaimed as Darcy lifted his head and gave an inquisitive snicker.

Martin undid the latch and gestured for Beth to go into the pen ahead of him.

Beth hesitated. "Are you sure it's safe to go in?"

"'Course," Martin said. "Are you chicken or what?"

Beth took two steps into the pen. Suddenly, she felt Martin shove her in the back and heard the gate slam shut.

She shot forward and almost went sprawling in the straw.

"You idiot!" she cried, turning around just in time to see Martin jogging away through the barn. "That's not funny!" she shouted after him.

There was a noise from behind her. Beth turned to see Darcy curling his lips and eyeing her suspiciously.

She swallowed. "N-nice goat."

Darcy lowered his head. He looked like he was going to charge!

Chapter
TWO

Beth's heart rose into her mouth.
Suddenly there was a dazzling flash of
gold light, and a big shower of bright
gold sparks sprinkled all around her and
Darcy. Blinded for a moment, she rubbed
her eyes. Beth tensed as she felt a peculiar
warm, tingly feeling down her spine.

When she could see again, she noticed
that Darcy was frozen where he stood,

and standing between the goat's legs was
a tiny fluffy black-and-white puppy with
enormous midnight-blue eyes. Specks
of gold dust seemed to be glimmering
around its fur.

"What's going on?" Beth exclaimed.

The tiny puppy drew itself up. "I am
Storm, of the Moon-claw pack. I have
arrived from a place that is far from here."

"Y-you can talk?" Beth gasped in total
amazement.

Suddenly, Beth had a realization. This was obviously another one of her cousin's practical jokes. She looked around, expecting Martin to jump out triumphantly.

But there was no sign of him. Beth slowly looked back to where Storm was blinking up at her, and Darcy was still standing as if he were carved from stone.

"I don't get this," she said, puzzled.

The fluffy black-and-white puppy took a few steps toward her on big soft paws that seemed too large for his tiny body. "I used my magic to stop this animal before it could hurt you," Storm woofed. "Who are you?"

"I'm B–Beth H–Hollis," Beth stammered.

Storm bowed his head. "I am honored to meet you, Beth."

Beth was still having trouble taking all of this in. "Um . . . me too. But . . . who are you? *What* are you?"

Storm didn't answer. Instead, there was another bright golden flash.

"Oh!" Beth found herself outside Darcy's pen. Behind her the goat snickered contentedly, and she heard him moving around in the straw as if nothing had happened.

Beth looked around for the puppy. But it had disappeared, and standing in its place outside the pen with her there crouched a magnificent young silver-gray wolf with glowing midnight-blue eyes. Large gold sparks glowed in the thick ruff around his neck.

Beth gasped, eyeing the wolf's sharp teeth. "Storm?"

"Yes, it is me, Beth. Do not be afraid," Storm said in a deep velvety growl.

Before Beth could get used to the sight of the amazing young wolf there was a final dazzling flash of gold light and Storm was once again a tiny fluffy black-and-white puppy.

"Wow! That's an amazing disguise.

No one would ever know you're a wolf!"
Beth exclaimed. "But who are you hiding
from?"

Storm began to tremble all over, and
his deep-blue eyes glowed with anger and
fear. "Shadow is a fierce lone wolf who
killed my father and all my brothers and
wounded my mother with his poisonous
bite. Now Shadow is looking for me. Can
you help me, Beth?"

"Of course I will!" Beth's soft heart
went out to him. Storm was impressive
as a young wolf, but he was adorable as
a tiny helpless puppy. She bent down to
pick him up. "I'll ask Auntie Em if you
can stay in my room," she said, petting his
soft little ears.

Storm leaned up to lick her chin.
"Thank you, Beth."

"Just wait until I tell Martin about you! He's going to be so jealous!"

"No, Beth! You can't tell anyone my secret!" Storm said, his tiny black-and-white face very serious.

Beth didn't want to do anything that would put her new friend in danger. Besides, she reasoned, Martin had been such a pain recently that he didn't deserve to know about Storm anyway. "Okay, then," she decided. "It's just you and me. I promise."

"Aren't you a little too old to be talking to an imaginary friend?" Martin said, suddenly appearing from behind the straw bales. His eyes widened when he saw Storm. "Where did that cute puppy come from?"

"I just found him. He said his name's—"

Beth stopped quickly as she realized that
she was going to have to be a lot more
careful about keeping Storm's secret. "I
mean I'm going to call him Storm."

Martin's face softened for an instant.
"Ella looked just like that when she was
a puppy. He must be a Border collie, too.
Let me hold him."

"I think I'll hold on to him. He's still a
little scared," Beth said.

Martin frowned. "No one would

think he's yours. This is my barn, so Storm
obviously belongs to me. Hand him over!"
he ordered.

Beth hesitated, annoyed at being
bossed around again. Martin didn't even
bother to ask if she was okay after he'd
shoved her into Darcy's pen.

"Do not worry, Beth. Do as he says,"
Storm woofed.

Beth blinked in astonishment. What
was Storm doing, talking to her when
Martin was so close? But her cousin didn't
seem to have noticed anything strange. *I
hope you know what you're doing, Storm*, she
thought as she reluctantly held him out
toward Martin.

Smiling triumphantly, Martin went to
grab Storm, but the moment he touched his
black-and-white fur he jumped backward.

"Ye-oww!" he yelled, shaking his hands in the air. "Something just stung me! Does he have a stinging bug in his fur or something?"

Beth pulled Storm back and held him closely again. "I'll take a look. Maybe you should go and ask Auntie Em for some antiseptic cream."

"Er . . . yeah." Martin nodded as he went off, still rubbing at his hands.

"Storm!" Beth scolded gently. "You

gave him a prick from your invisible gold sparks, didn't you?"

Storm's blue eyes twinkled mischievously. "I think I may have made them a bit too sharp. But the feeling will soon wear off," he woofed.

"Serves Martin right. Maybe he'll think twice before grabbing you again! But how come he didn't hear you speak to me just now?" Beth asked, puzzled.

"I used my magic, so that only you can hear me." Storm snuggled up in Beth's arms.

"You can do that? So I can hear you, but everyone else just hears you barking? Cool!" Beth kissed the top of his soft little head. "Let's go and find Auntie Em. Breakfast should be almost ready. I bet you're hungry after your long journey."

Storm's tummy rumbled and he gave an eager little bark.

As Beth went toward the farmhouse, she smiled. Her boring two weeks at Tail End Farm looked like they were going to be a lot more fun with Storm around!

Chapter
THREE

"I wonder where he came from,"
Emily said thoughtfully after Beth finished
telling her about Storm. "We're pretty far
from any houses out here."

Beth looked across to where Storm
was chomping on a dish of dog food. Ella,
the old collie, lay curled in her basket
watching the puppy.

"I bet Storm was abandoned. His

owners were probably hoping some kind person would give him a home. Like you, Auntie Em," Beth said hopefully.

"I really hate people who treat animals like that," Martin said.

"Me too!" Beth said with feeling. It was the first time she and Martin had agreed on anything.

They all sat at the kitchen table, eating their huge farmhouse breakfasts and drinking big mugs of tea.

"I'm not sure it's a good time to have a stray puppy getting under everyone's feet," Beth's uncle said. "We're very busy on the farm and no one has time to train him. Maybe we should take Storm straight to the pet care center."

Beth's heart pounded. He couldn't mean it! She just found Storm—she couldn't bear to lose her new friend so quickly.

Suddenly Ella gave a rusty-sounding bark. She got up and limped stiffly over to Storm. The tiny puppy whined softly, wagging his tail and wriggling his fat little body as the old dog bent down and gave him an experimental sniff. Ella's eyes softened and she began licking Storm's head.

Martin's face lit up. "Look at that! Ella's telling us that she'll keep Storm in check. She won't let him be a pest around the farm. Way to go, old girl!"

Everyone laughed.

Beth looked at her uncle and aunt. "So, can Storm stay? He can live in my room and I'll take him home when Mom and Dad come to get me," she pleaded.

"In that case, it's fine with me. If it's okay with you, Emily," Oliver said to his wife.

Beth's aunt gave a questionable smile, but she nodded.

Beth went over and hugged her aunt and uncle. "Yay! Thanks a million!"

She felt so happy that she was even ready to forgive Martin for playing mean tricks on her, but there was still one thing she wanted to mention to him first.

Beth waited until she, Martin, Storm, and Ella were walking across the fields before bringing the subject up. "I think you should apologize for pushing me into Darcy's pen. It was a mean thing to do," she exclaimed.

Martin's eyes widened. "Are you still talking about that? Can't you take a joke? Girls *always* make such a big deal out of everything."

"Yes, because boys do such stupid things!" Beth replied. "I thought Darcy was going to charge at me. If it hadn't been for St—Anyway, I was lucky to get out without getting hurt."

But Martin wasn't listening. He had turned around to wait for Ella, who was lagging behind. The old collie was walking stiffly with her head drooping. "Come on, girl!" he called fondly.

At the sound of his voice, Ella tried to quicken her step, but her back legs gave way and she sat down.

"She's been doing that more and more lately," Martin said, frowning.

Beth's anger with Martin melted away as her heart filled with sadness at the sight of the sick old dog.

Storm glanced up at her with softly glowing eyes. "I will fetch Ella!" he woofed gently.

Beth stood beside Martin and they watched Storm bound down the field. As soon as Storm reached the old sheepdog, he barked encouragingly and licked Ella's gray muzzle. When she just lay there panting, Storm crouched down onto his front paws and stuck his bottom in the air, inviting her to play chase.

Martin smiled at the cute puppy's antics. "You're wasting your time, Storm. Ella's running around days are *well* over!" he called, but then his face fell and his eyes looked sad and troubled.

Beth reached out to touch his arm.

"I'm okay. Don't make a scene!" Martin said, rubbing a sleeve across his face.

Beth saw Storm running back and forth in front of Ella, woofing gently to encourage her until she finally heaved herself to her feet. As the old collie limped up the field, Storm ambled alongside her, keeping pace on his short legs.

"Here she comes. Good girl," Martin said, petting Ella's ears.

"Thanks, Storm," Beth whispered to him. "Martin might be the most annoying person in the universe, but he really loves Ella."

The four of them slowly walked back to the farmyard in silence. As they came through the gate into the yard, Martin turned to Beth. "Do you want to see the dairy?" he said more cheerfully.

Beth shrugged. "I don't care. But I thought we weren't allowed in there without permission."

"No problem. I told Mom we might go in and she was cool with it." Martin opened the door of a brick building, next to the barn. "But dogs are definitely not allowed. Stay, Ella," he ordered.

Ella sat down obediently.

"Will you wait here, please, Storm?"

Beth whispered, so Martin couldn't hear. "I won't be long."

Storm immediately sat down next to Ella and lay with his nose on his paws.

Martin smiled. "Storm really catches on quickly, doesn't he? Look how he copies what Ella does. He's one bright puppy!"

Beth smiled to herself. If only Martin knew how right he was!

Inside the dairy it was cool and really clean. Beth walked around, looking at the white work surfaces, shiny metal equipment, and huge fridges, being careful not to touch anything.

But Martin was just the opposite. "I haven't been in here for so long. I forgot that some of this stuff's pretty high-tech. I wonder what these do." He began turning some dials on a big drum-shaped machine.

There was an ominous glugging noise.

"Should you be playing with that?"
Beth asked worriedly.

Martin grinned. "You're such a
scaredy-cat. Don't panic. I'm putting the
settings back to what they were." He
turned the dial again and the glugging
noise got louder.

Gloop. Gloop. Whoosh!

Suddenly a fountain of milk gushed
out of a narrow chute and poured onto
the floor.

"Oh no!" Martin cried, frantically
working, but the milk only sprayed out
faster.

Beth stood there in horror as a rising
tide of milk swirled around her boots. "Do
something, Martin!"

"I'm trying to!" Martin's face was bright red.

The door banged open and Emily Badby rushed into the dairy. Taking in the situation with one look, she marched over to the machine and adjusted the dials. Seconds later, the flow of milk slowed and then stopped.

Emily turned around with a furious look on her face.

"Beth told me to do it!" Martin cried, before his mom could speak.

Beth's jaw dropped. "No, I didn't!"

Martin smirked. "Yes, you did! Don't try and squirm your way out of it—"

"Be quiet! Both of you," Emily snapped. "I'm very disappointed in you both. You're not even supposed to be in here without permission!"

Beth glared furiously at Martin. She was really tempted to tell her aunt how he had lied about having permission to come in here, but she'd never been a tattletale and she wasn't about to start now.

"You know the house rules perfectly well, Martin. Besides, Beth is our guest," Emily said stiffly, still furious. "What do you have to say for yourself?"

Martin shrugged. "Chill out, Mom! Don't have a major panic attack! It's only a little milk. It won't take long to clean up."

"You think so?" Emily's face darkened. "Stay there, you two! Don't you dare move!" She sloshed through the milk and opened a cabinet. "Here!" She thrust mops and buckets at Martin and Beth. "I want

that floor spotless. Do you hear me? I'd
stand and watch you, but I have to go
out now. I'll be back in an hour, though,
to check up on you. And if you touch
anything else, Martin Badby, you'll . . .
you'll be in big trouble!"

She stormed out, and a few seconds
later Beth heard a car start up and drive
away.

"Oh gosh!" Beth said, letting out a
huge sigh of relief. She'd never seen her
aunt so angry. "I thought she was going to
explode!"

"Oh, Mom's never angry for long.
She'll forget all about it by this evening.
You don't mind cleaning up by yourself,
do you? I just remembered I've got
something important to talk to Dad
about," Martin said, splashing milk

everywhere as he went toward the door.

"Hey! Come back—" Beth cried, but Martin had already left.

Her spirits sank as she looked down at the lake of milk. It was everywhere: under the work surfaces, sloshing around the machinery, and even leaking out under the door into the yard. She hardly knew where to begin.

"Thanks for nothing, Martin," she grumbled, angry that she'd bothered to save him from being in even more trouble with her aunt.

"I will help you, Beth!" Storm woofed eagerly from the open doorway.

Beth felt a warm prickling sensation down her spine. Something very strange was about to happen.

Chapter
FOUR

Big gold sparks ignited in Storm's fluffy black-and-white fur, and his ears and tail crackled with electricity.

Storm raised a big black front paw, and a spurt of golden sparks shot out and whooshed around the dairy. They zizzed around like a swarm of busy worker bees.

Beth heard a series of faint pops as a shimmering army of mops appeared out of thin air and stood at attention. As if at an invisible signal, they began mopping the floor up and down in neat rows. In perfect time, they squeezed their milky heads into each bucket in turn. *Swish! Swoosh!*

"This is great!" Beth said, clapping her hands with glee as the rows of mops did their work.

In no time at all, the dairy floor was spotless. The magic mops stood at

attention once more and then disappeared in a final cascade of golden sparks.

"Wow! Thanks, Storm, that was awesome!" Beth went over and gave him a cuddle.

"You are welcome," Storm barked happily. "But I saw Martin going into the house. Why didn't he help you?"

"That's what I want to know," Beth said angrily. "He made some lame excuse about talking to his dad about something. I've had just about enough of my annoying cousin. Come on, Storm, let's go and find him. I've got a few things I want to say to him!"

Storm yapped in agreement.

As Beth charged into the house with Storm toward the living room, she heard Uncle Ollie's voice coming through the open door and stopped in her tracks.

"It's really not fair to let Ella go on like this. She's in pain and she can barely move around. I think it's time we called the vet and put her to sleep," he was saying.

"No! Please wait, Dad. Let's leave her for just a little longer," Martin pleaded, sounding as if he was very close to tears.

"I'm sorry, Martin. I know you love Ella, but I'm not prepared to let any animal suffer, however hard it is for you to accept. We have to think what's best for Ella. Why don't we talk about it again tomorrow. All right?" Oliver Badby said gently.

"Okay. But I'm not changing my mind about calling the vet and you can't make me!" Martin said in a choked voice.

Beth didn't wait to hear the rest of
the conversation. She already felt a little
guilty for listening. "Come on, Storm," she
whispered, tiptoeing away.

Storm trotted at her heel as she went
into the kitchen. Beth felt her anger drain
away again, just like when they were in
the field earlier. However annoying her

cousin was, she wouldn't wish that on anyone.

"Martin was actually telling the truth this time. He really did want to talk to his dad about something important. Ella must be very sick if Uncle Ollie thinks the vet should put her to sleep. Poor old girl," she said to Storm.

Storm nodded, his midnight-blue eyes sad.

Ella was curled up in her basket in the warm alcove. As Beth bent down to pet her, the old dog's tail thumped against the floor.

Beth felt tears stinging her eyes. "It's a shame that Ella's in such pain. If she wasn't, she'd be able to enjoy a few more months with Martin."

Storm pricked his ears. "I might be able to help!"

Beth blinked at him. "Really? Can you use your magic to make her young again?" she asked hopefully.

"I am sorry, Beth. No magic can do that," Storm woofed gently. He padded over and stood in front of Ella.

Once again, Beth felt the warm tingling sensation down her spine.

Big gold sparks ignited in Storm's fluffy black-and-white fur and the tips of his ears sparked with magical power. She watched as he huffed out a warm glittery breath.

A shimmering golden mist surrounded the old collie. For a few seconds, pinpricks of gold danced all around her like miniature fireflies and then they sank into

Ella's dull fur and disappeared.

Beth waited expectantly, but nothing happened. Ella looked just the same, with her gray muzzle and faded eyes.

Storm's magic didn't seem to have worked.

"Never mind. You tried. I guess magic can't be expected to do everything," Beth said to Storm, trying hard to hide her disappointment as the last golden spark faded from Ella's fur. "Let's go into the living room and find Martin. He's

probably feeling really upset. Maybe we can cheer him up."

Storm had a gleam in his eye, but he just nodded. "You have a very kind heart, Beth."

"Anyone would do the same," Beth said, blushing. She always got embarrassed when people gave her compliments.

Martin was lying on the sofa. Behind it, Beth could see the cabinet displaying the cups and trophies her uncle had won in plowing competitions.

Oliver Badby sat at the table, working at the computer. He looked up and smiled as Beth and Storm came in. "Hello. What have you two been up to?"

"We . . . I've finished cleaning up all the milk in the dairy. I thought Martin might like to go out with us or something," Beth said.

Her uncle frowned and glanced at Martin. "What's that about milk?"

"Er . . . nothing!" Martin said hurriedly, getting up in a rush and pushing Beth out. "Come on, Beth. Let's go and see if Mom needs any help with her shopping."

"But she's not even back yet . . ." Beth protested, shaking off his arm.

"Duh! I know that! But Dad doesn't, does he?" Martin scoffed. "And why did you have to mention the milk?"

But once in the hall, his shoulders slumped. "Dad's been talking about taking Ella to the vet, to . . . to—"

"I know. I heard you talking to him," Beth interrupted, feeling a lump rise in her throat. "I'm so sorry."

Martin shuffled his feet. "Yeah, well.
I know Ella's old and everything and I'm
not ready to let her go, but Dad could
be ..." He lifted his head and looked
past Beth into the kitchen. She saw an
expression of complete amazement come
over his face. "I don't believe it!"

"What?" Beth whipped around and

saw Ella padding out of the kitchen.
The old dog was moving easily. Her coat
looked glossy and her eyes were bright
and alert.

Ella trotted up to Martin and jumped
up to be petted. "Woof!" she barked
happily, wagging her tail and giving him a
wide doggy grin.

"Look at her! It's like a miracle. She's
not even limping!" Martin threw his arms
around Ella and hugged her, burying his
face in her fur.

Ella barked, licking him all over his
face.

"Just wait until Dad sees her! There's
no way he'll be taking her to the vet
now!" Martin's face was lit up like a
Halloween pumpkin.

Beth beamed with joy as she watched

the two of them. She bent down to pet
Storm. "Thanks again, Storm. This time
from Martin and Ella. They're going
to have a great summer together," she
whispered.

Storm wagged his little tail happily.

Chapter
FIVE

"Ella seems to have found a new
best friend since that puppy arrived,"
Emily Badby said as she was clearing away
lunch the following day.

Beth was helping her aunt load the
dishwasher. She smiled, wishing that
everyone knew just how true that was!
But, of course, she would never tell them
or anyone else how magical Storm was.

Oliver Badby was finishing a cup of tea, and Martin had just come back into the kitchen after taking some food scraps outside to the pigpen.

Storm was stretched out under the table. Suddenly his eyes flashed with mischief. Leaping out, he ran around the huge farmhouse table, his ears laid back and his tail streaming behind him.

Across the room in her bed, Ella's ears pricked up. With a spring in her step, she shot toward the silly puppy and started chasing him. Storm suddenly swerved, leaped into her empty bed, and threw himself down. Ella jumped straight in after him. Seconds later, the two of them were curled up together, licking each other.

Everyone laughed.

"That's one way to sneak into a warm

bed! You know, Ella and Storm could
almost be a mother and her puppy,"
Martin said fondly.

Then they heard the rumbling sound
of a heavy truck pulling up outside in
the yard. Martin ran to the window and
looked out.

"It's here, Dad! The Fergy's arrived!"
he shouted, dashing outside.

Beth's uncle and aunt went outside to

look. Beth followed curiously, wondering
what was going on.

A large flatbed truck stood in the yard.
On the back of it, there was a tomato-red
tractor. Oliver went to speak to the truck
driver, and then they began the unloading.
A few minutes later, the red tractor stood
in the yard.

Martin walked around it, his eyes
shining. "It's supercool, isn't it?"

"I guess it's okay," Beth said, shrugging.
She couldn't see what was so exciting
about a boring old farm machine.

"Okay?" Martin gave her an
incredulous look. "Are you kidding? That's
a 1952 Massey Ferguson tractor."

Beth wasn't impressed. "It's kind of
old, isn't it? Does it still work?"

Her uncle chuckled. "Fergy's going

to work very well. Wait until you see her pulling a plow. She's going to help me win the cup in the vintage class at the plowing competition in a few weeks."

"Dad's county champion at plowing," Martin said proudly.

To Beth, winning things for making straight lines down a field seemed like a very weird thing to do. *Don't they watch any TV around here?* she thought.

Martin saw the scornful look on her face. He blushed. "There's a lot of skill involved in plowing, you know. Dad lets me try sometimes and I'm getting really good at it," he boasted. "I'm going to get a license when I'm fourteen. Then I can compete, too!"

"You're doing all right, but you'll need a lot more practice first," his dad said.

"I know that," Martin said in a sulky voice.

Oliver patted his son on the shoulder. "Fergy could use a wash and brush up. She's pretty dusty after her journey. Any volunteers?"

Martin's head came up. "Beth and I will do it. Won't we, Beth?"

Beth frowned. Cleaning a tractor was definitely not on the top of her "fun to do" list. It was right at the bottom, next

to cleaning smelly sneakers. But Martin
seemed in an unusually good mood, so she
nodded.

"Okay. I don't mind." *But if he starts
bossing me around again, I'm leaving him to
do it*, she thought.

Beth helped Martin collect buckets,
sponges, and cleaning liquid. Storm came
outside and lay down with his chin resting
on his paws as she and Martin started
work.

"There's all kinds of plowing, you
know. Tractor-trailed, mounted, reversible.
You have to be very skilled to work a plot
and make perfect ins and outs," Martin
explained enthusiastically as he sponged
soapy water over Fergy's bright-red
hood. "They have world championship
competitions. One day Dad might be

good enough to participate."

Beth didn't reply. She was scrubbing hard at a greasy mark on Fergy's red grill.

"Hey! Are you listening? Or are you ignoring me on purpose?" Martin flicked soapy water at her.

"Who said that?" Beth joked and flicked water back at him.

Martin's eyes gleamed mischievously. "Oh yeah!"

Beth dodged out of the way as another sponge full of water flew toward her. "Missed!" she teased.

Laughing, they flicked soapy water back and forth.

Beth giggled as she pushed her damp hair out of her eyes and crouched behind the tractor. She was smaller than Martin and managed to avoid getting too wet, but most of her soapy flicks found their mark.

Martin's T-shirt was soon drenched.
"Right! Now you're in for it!" He
grabbed the whole bucket and lifted it
into the air.

"Don't you dare!" Beth shrieked
breathlessly.

As she went to flick more water at

Martin, a tiny shower of golden sparks
crackled around her hand and tingled
against her fingers. The soapy sponge
shot out of her hand. It zoomed through
the air with perfect aim and splatted in
Martin's face.

"Phoof!" Martin spluttered. He took
a step backward and slipped over onto
his backside, tipping the entire bucket of
water all over himself.

Beth cracked up laughing. She was
helpless. She glanced across at Storm, who
wore a wide doggy grin, and wagged her
finger at him, scolding him gently.

"Sorry, Beth. I thought he was going
to hurt you!" Storm yapped.

Scowling, Martin slowly got up. His
dark hair was plastered to his head, and
water was dripping off the end of his nose.

Beth tried to stop laughing at the look on Martin's face, but her mouth kept twitching. "You should see yourself," she gasped, holding her ribs.

Suddenly Martin burst out laughing, too. "That was a great shot—for a girl! Come on, let's get some clean water."

Beth went with him to fill her bucket from the outside tap. Staying at Tail End Farm was starting to feel a lot better these days.

She was amazed at Martin. This was the most friendly he'd been since she arrived. And all because they'd had a water fight and she'd beaten him. *I'll never understand boys*, she thought as they finished cleaning the tractor.

Chapter
SIX

Beth stood in the barn beside her aunt and watched her milking the goats. Storm was sprawled on a pile of clean straw beside the pens.

Beth sighed. It had rained almost every day since she'd been here. Heavy rain was drumming on the roof once again. "I'm getting fed up with this terrible weather," she complained.

Emily smiled. "You learn to deal
with it when you work on a farm. But
the goats really hate the cold and the
wet. That's why I brought them into the
barn, but I'd hoped they could go out in
their field again by now." She looked at
her niece's sad face. "Do you want to try
milking?"

"I don't know," Beth said doubtfully.

"Come on. Don't be shy. Stand here.
It's not very difficult and Daisy's a good

milker," Emily encouraged. She showed Beth how to take a firm but gentle hold and squeeze down with one finger at a time.

Beth took a deep breath and rested one shoulder against Daisy's flank. She followed instructions, a bit awkwardly at first. To her surprise, the milk began to flow into the bucket.

"Hey! I'm doing it!" she cried delightedly.

In a few minutes Beth felt like an expert. She filled a bucket and then strained the milk into the metal churn, feeling really pleased with her success. "That was great. Maybe I'll ask Mom and Dad if we can have some goats. It would save Dad moaning about having to dig up all the weeds, and we'd have tons of milk to give to all our friends."

"Hmm. Remember that you'd have to milk them twice a day, summer and winter, seven days a week, in all kinds of weather, just like I do," her aunt cautioned, smiling.

Beth raised her eyebrows. "On second thought, I think I'll stick to milk in cartons and leave the weeds to Dad!"

Her aunt laughed.

A loud triumphant braying came from the back of the barn. There was a stamping and clattering, followed by a rustling noise.

"Darcy?! What's he doing?" Beth asked.

"It sounds like he's jumped out of his pen—again," her aunt sighed. "That goat's a real menace. He's been cooped up for too long because of all this rain and he's got energy to spare. It's going to be really hard to catch him."

"Can I help you?" Beth offered.

"You could go and see where Darcy's gone, if you like, while I close the barn door so he can't escape," her aunt said.

"I will find Darcy!" Storm barked, darting to the back of the barn.

Beth hurried after him. As she reached the big stack of straw bales near the goat's pen, she spotted Darcy standing right on the very top of them.

"Look at him! He thinks he's the king of the castle!" Beth said.

Looking down his haughty nose, Darcy snickered as if he agreed. He looked very pleased with himself for having climbed up so high.

Storm wagged his tail and then jumped up onto his back legs and put his front paws on the bottom bale.

"Gr-oof!" his bright eyes flashed playfully.

"Watch out, Storm. That stack looks a little wobbly—" Beth began, but before she could finish her sentence, Darcy flexed his powerful back legs and did an almighty leap in the air, right over Beth and Storm's heads—and then everything seemed to happen all at once.

The top straw bale shook wildly from the force of Darcy's takeoff and slowly began to tip forward.

Beth's eyes widened in horror. Storm had turned his head to watch Darcy land on the barn floor a few feet away and hadn't noticed the danger. The bale was about to fall and land on him!

Without a second thought, Beth threw
herself forward. Her fingers just touched
Storm's fluffy black-and-white fur and she
managed to grab him. Holding him close
to her chest Beth rolled out of the way
just in time. The heavy bale crashed to the

ground, and she felt the rush of dusty air as it missed them both by a fraction of an inch.

Beth let out a shaky sigh of relief. Still holding Storm, she pushed herself slowly to her feet. "Are you all right?" she asked the shocked little puppy.

"Yes. You saved me, Beth. Thank you," Storm woofed, reaching up to lick her chin.

"I couldn't bear anything happening to you," Beth said as she petted Storm's soft ears. She felt a surge of affection for her tiny friend.

Glancing down the barn, Beth saw that her aunt had managed to get a rope on a subdued-looking Darcy and was leading him back to his pen. She frowned when she reached Beth and Storm and saw the straw bale on the floor nearby. "I thought I heard something fall, but I couldn't be sure with all the noise Darcy was making. Are you okay? You're lucky you weren't badly hurt," she said.

"Oh, it missed us by miles," Beth said lightly, not wanting to worry her aunt.

"Thank goodness for that!" Emily said, relieved. "I'm responsible for you while you're here, and your mom and dad wouldn't be very happy with me if you had an accident. I'll get Oliver to come and fix that stack. Just let me tether this naughty goat in his pen first. He's full of surprises."

Beth bit back a grin. *He's not the only one!* she thought.

"I'm sorry, Martin, I don't have time to go out with you today. Maybe tomorrow. I'm planning to clear the unused part of the top field and use that for practicing plowing, but I can't promise when I'll get around to it," Oliver was saying.

"Aw, Da-ad. You've already been out on Fergy a couple of times. When am I going to get the chance to take a drive?"

Beth sat in the window seat in the

living room with Storm curled on a cushion beside her. Her uncle and cousin were in the yard outside. Their voices floated in through the open window. "Martin's obsessed with that dumb old red tractor, even though Uncle Ollie told him it's too big for him to drive by himself."

Storm's ears twitched and he gave a sleepy nod, tired out from all the excitement in the barn earlier.

Two minutes later, Martin burst into the room and threw himself down next to Beth.

"Watch it! You almost sat on Storm!" Beth complained.

"Sorry, Storm." Martin petted Storm's fluffy black-and-white fur absently. "Dad's being a big pain! He won't let me near

Fergy unless he's with me. I know I can handle driving her by myself, but he won't believe me," he grumbled.

Beth wisely chose to stay silent on the subject. "It finally stopped raining. Why don't we walk into the village with Storm and Ella?" she suggested, trying to cheer him up.

Martin's lip curled. "Go shopping? I'd rather watch paint dry. I'm going to take Ella for a long walk over the fields. By myself," he said rudely.

Beth got the message. She didn't bother to tell him that she was about to suggest that they go to the new sports center. "Suit yourself." She shrugged, got up, and called to Storm to follow her.

"Where are you going?" Martin asked, frowning.

Beth turned to him and tapped the side of her nose with one finger in what she knew was an annoying way.

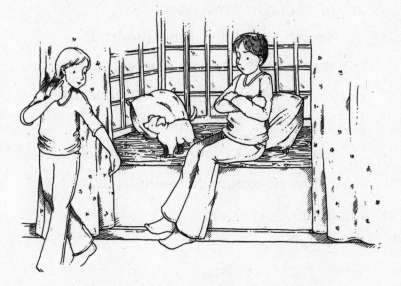

Martin threw up his hands, got up, and stormed out, muttering about "stupid annoying girls" under his breath.

"Oh well. Martin's back to his usual self. His good mood didn't last long, did it?" Beth said to Storm. "But I'm getting used to him now and I don't mind it so much. I think he just likes complaining!"

Storm nodded, blinking up at her with bright midnight-blue eyes.

Beth changed her mind about the sports center. "We'll go to the village by ourselves. I bet they have a pet shop that sells dog treats," she decided.

Storm yelped excitedly, almost falling over his own paws as he bounded out of the door.

Chapter
SEVEN

Emily Badby had been baking bread
all morning, and the whole farmhouse
smelled wonderful.

Beth sat in the cozy kitchen, reading
a new computer magazine she'd bought
at the village shop. Storm was curled
up under the table, chewing on a bone-
shaped dog chew, and Beth could feel the
tiny puppy's warmth against her feet.

It had just been raining again, but a watery sun was now beginning to push through the clouds.

Suddenly the faint sound of barking and growling interrupted Beth's peaceful morning. She tensed up, listening hard. It seemed to be coming from far away, but then the noise stopped and Beth thought she must have been mistaken. Her aunt didn't seem to have noticed anything.

"Where's Martin?" Beth asked.

"Up at the top field. His dad's starting to clear it with Fergy and the old plow. Ella's with him," Emily replied.

Making sure her aunt wasn't looking, Beth leaned over to whisper to Storm. "I'll take you for a walk up there later. It's no good waiting for Martin and Ella to come back here. Wild horses wouldn't drag him

away if Uncle Ollie's plowing."

There was no reply.

Frowning, Beth bent over and looked under the table. Storm was gone, leaving the half-eaten dog chew lying there.

That was odd. He'd never run off without telling her where he was going before. She got up and went to look for him.

Storm wasn't in the living room or
any of the other downstairs rooms. She
went up to her bedroom, expecting to
find him curled up on her blanket, but he
wasn't there either.

"Storm?" she said, beginning to feel
concerned.

A faint sound came from under her
pillows. Beth smiled and pulled back the
top of the blanket to reveal a little black-
and-white tail. "What's this, hide-and-
seek—" she began, but stopped at the
sight of Storm trembling all over. "What's
wrong? Are you sick?" she
asked worriedly.

Storm squirmed farther into the
pillows. "I sense that Shadow knows
where I am. He will send his magic, so
that any dogs that are nearby will attack

me," he said in a muffled little whine.

"Oh no! That must have been what I heard. We need to find you a better hiding place. Maybe the barn or . . . or . . ." Beth tried to think of somewhere safe.

"It is no use, Beth," Storm whimpered, his deep-blue eyes as dull as stones. "Leave me here for a while, please. Any dogs looking for me may pass by."

"All right. If that's what you want," Beth said. She had a sudden thought. "What about Ella? Will Shadow's magic work on her, too?" She felt horrified that the gentle old collie might become Storm's enemy.

"No. I have already used my magic to help her. That will protect Ella from Shadow's evil ways," Storm whined before he burrowed right under the pillows and curled up into a tight little ball.

Beth gently gathered his tail in, replaced the blanket, and tucked it tightly around him. No one would know there was anything under the pillow. She went out quietly, hoping that Storm's plan would work. She couldn't bear to think

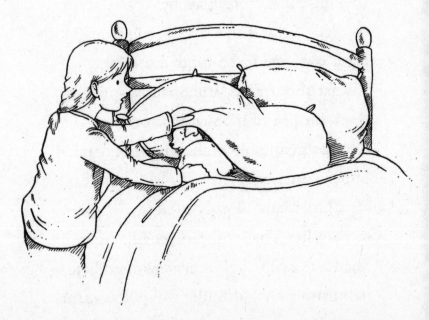

of her friend having to leave suddenly
without warning.

Beth could hardly eat any lunch
because she was so worried about Storm.
She nibbled on a few mouthfuls of salad
and cauliflower and then asked if she
could leave the table.

"Are you feeling all right?" her aunt
asked.

"Fine, thanks. I'm just not very
hungry," Beth replied.

Martin glanced at Beth in concern and
seemed about to say something, but then
he changed his mind. He finished eating
and jumped up from the table.

"Why don't you and Storm come up
to the top field before lunch and see how
Dad and I are doing? We've cleared a lot

of it already. I'm going up there again now with Ella. You could come with us, if you like."

"I might. I'll ... um ... follow you up there in a minute," Beth murmured absently.

"Whatever," Martin muttered.

When he and Ella had left, Beth went into the hall with a heavy heart. She was dreading going upstairs to her bedroom. Would Storm still be here or had her friend already left forever?

Suddenly, a tiny fluffy black-and-white figure came bounding down the stairs. "Hello, Beth," Storm barked happily.

"Storm! You're still here!" Beth cried, overjoyed, throwing her arms around him.

Storm yapped and licked her face, his tail moving wildly. His midnight-blue eyes were as bright as a moonlit sky and he seemed completely back to his usual self. "I cannot sense any strange dogs nearby, so they must have gone away. But if they return I might have to leave at once. We might not have time to say good-bye."

"I understand," Beth said, hardly taking this in. She just wanted to enjoy every single moment of the time they could spend together now.

She secretly hoped that Storm would stay with her forever, even though she knew he must someday return to help his injured mother and lead the Moon-claw wolf pack.

Beth decided to talk about something else. "Do you want to go watch Uncle Ollie giving Martin some plowing practice? It'll probably be really boring," she said, making a face.

Storm's cute face lit up, as it always did at any chance of a walk.

* ⭐ *

Where's Uncle Ollie? Beth wondered as they walked toward the top field. She could see the red tractor and the plow mounted behind it, but only Martin and Ella stood beside it.

Storm was trotting beside her with his nose sniffing around on the ground.

Martin waved. "Hi! I didn't think you'd come," he shouted, sounding surprised and pleased.

Ella spotted Storm. She wagged her tail and trotted over, barking a greeting.

"I thought we might as well. Storm loves playing with Ella," Beth said, smiling at the dogs.

"Great. Now you can see what plowing's all about. Watch this," Martin called out. Leaping into Fergy's seat he started the engine and moved forward.

"Martin, don't! You're not supposed to be doing that!" Beth said worriedly, remembering her uncle's strict rules about Martin only driving under his supervision.

"I know what I'm doing!" Martin said huffily. "Anyway, I'll only plow a couple of furrows. Dad just went down to the barn for a can of lubricating oil—he'll never

know. Unless you decide to tell him," he
said, looking harshly at her.

"Thanks a lot. You should know
by now that I don't tell!" Beth said
indignantly.

Martin looked uncomfortable
and then he gave a grin and nodded.
Concentrating hard, he held the large
steering wheel steady as the red tractor
trundled slowly along, pulling the plow
behind it. As he moved forward, the
weedy ground was turned over and the
soil curved away from the plow's metal
moldboards in rich brown waves.

Despite herself, Beth was fascinated by
watching the furrows form. Martin leaned
over to watch the back wheels, making
sure he kept driving in a perfectly straight
line. The new brown furrow folded itself

over and was laid neatly next to one previously made.

Beth realized that plowing took a lot of skill. "You're pretty good at this, aren't you?" she said, impressed.

Martin threw her a smile over his shoulder, obviously enjoying himself and pleased by her praise. "I'm not bad. But then I was taught by an expert. My dad!"

Suddenly Storm's head came up and his midnight-blue eyes flashed. Barking shrilly, he raced forward and began darting back and forth in front of Fergy's front wheels. "Stop! Stop!" he barked urgently.

"Martin! Watch out for Storm!" Beth cried.

"Why's he doing that? Make him stop!" Martin shouted.

Beth frowned. It wasn't like Storm

to do something so dangerous without a good reason. But she was too worried about him getting hurt to try and figure out what that was.

"Come here, Storm! You'll get hurt!" she shouted.

But Storm seemed determined. Barking frantically, he ran even closer to the tractor's ridged tires, snapping at them and growling. One of the wheels passed by him closely, missing him by a fraction.

As a stone flew out and hit him, Storm gave a loud yelp.

"Martin! Look out!" Beth screamed, thinking that Storm was about to be run over.

Panicking, Martin jerked the tractor's steering wheel to avoid the tiny puppy. Fergy rolled to a halt. Martin turned off the engine and jumped down.

"Look at that furrow. It's all messed up now. That stupid puppy made me mess up!" he fumed.

Storm stood by, panting heavily, his little sides heaving.

"Hang on! What's that? Look!" Beth interrupted, pointing at something half

buried in a weedy grass ditch that Martin
had been just about to plow over. As
Beth leaned over for a closer look, her
heart missed a beat. "I think it might be a
firecracker!"

Chapter
EIGHT

"Don't be crazy!" Martin said to Beth, walking over to take a look, but the moment he saw the metal object he frowned. "Oh! You're right. It does look like a firecracker. But it's probably been there for a while. Look, it's all shriveled and dented. I bet it's harmless."

"Storm didn't seem to think so," Beth reminded him.

Martin hesitated, chewing at his lip.

Beth guessed that he was worried about getting into trouble for driving the tractor. "Martin, this is an emergency. We have to go and tell Uncle Ollie—now!" she said.

"You're right," Martin decided. "Come on!"

Beth didn't need to be told twice. She

bent down to pick up Storm and then
turned on her heel and ran. Martin and
Ella leaped after her and they all hurried
back toward the farm as fast as they could.

Luckily Oliver was just coming out
of the barn with an oil can. He raised his
eyebrows when they raced straight up
to him. "Where's the fire?" he joked, but
his face grew serious as Martin and Beth
began explaining.

"Good job, you two. You did the right
thing. Firecrackers need expert handling.
I'll call the emergency services and then
alert the neighbors." He took his cell
phone out of his jacket pocket and dialed.
"Martin, will you go into the house and
tell your mom, please?"

Martin nodded, his face now pale with
worry.

Beth realized that her cousin had only just begun to grasp how serious this really was. Now that they were all a safe distance from the firecracker, she found herself shaking as it all sank in.

"Thank goodness you sensed the firecracker was there. You were very brave to get so close to the tractor and risk getting hurt," she whispered to Storm.

"I had to stop Martin somehow. We were too close for me to use my magic. Martin would have seen, but I could not risk anyone getting hurt," Storm woofed gently.

Beth and Storm stood in the yard with Martin, Ella, and her aunt as noisy police cars and fire engines arrived. Farm workers and their families began gathering, too.

Beth looked toward the top field, where the lights from half a dozen police cars were now flashing. She could see at least four fire engines. Bright-yellow hazard tape had been put up all around the site of the firecracker and across the field entrance.

"If it hadn't been for Storm, I'd have plowed right over that firecracker," Martin said. He bent down to pat Storm's head. "Thanks, boy. You might have just saved my life."

"You are welcome, Martin," Storm barked, wagging his tail, but of course only Beth could hear him speaking.

She beamed down at Storm, feeling very proud of her brave little friend.

Oliver came up and put a hand on his son's shoulder. "I should ground you for a

week for driving Fergy when I specifically
told you not to!" he said sternly.

"It wasn't my fault. Beth . . ." Martin
started to make another excuse to get
himself out of trouble, but then he seemed
to think otherwise and hung his head.
"Beth told me I shouldn't be driving
Fergy by myself and she was right. I'm
sorry, Dad."

"You always are," Oliver sighed. "But
on this occasion it was lucky for all of us
that things turned out this way. If I'd have
been plowing and not you, I probably
wouldn't have seen the firecracker until it
was too late."

Martin looked subdued as he took this
in and realized what it could have meant.
He was silent for a moment, and then he
brightened. "So I'm not in all that much

trouble after all. Cool!"

"I give up!" His dad shook his head slowly and rolled his eyes.

"Look, someone in the field's waving a red flag," Beth noticed.

Just then Oliver's cell phone rang. He answered it and then spoke in a loud voice. "Listen up, everyone. There's going

to be a controlled explosion in a few minutes. We shouldn't be alarmed. We're safe here."

Whump! A loud bang split the air.

Despite the early warning, Beth almost jumped out of her skin as the explosion echoed in her ears. An enormous spray of dark soil shot out in all directions and a thick dark smoke drifted upward.

"Yay! Way to go!" Martin shouted.

Everyone clapped and cheered. The danger was over.

"There'll be no more plowing in that field until the firemen have declared it safe. Do you hear me, Martin?" Oliver said.

"I wouldn't go up there now if you paid me," Martin said.

Beth could see that he meant it this time. Martin really seemed to be changing and Beth realized that she'd actually grown to like her grumpy cousin during her time at Tail End Farm!

"If you'd all like to come into the house I'll make coffee, and there's freshly made cake," Emily called out to everyone.

People began filing into the farmhouse. Martin called Ella and they followed them in. Beth was about to go in, too, when Storm suddenly barked with terror and ran toward the barn.

Beth heard a fierce growl behind her and looked around. She spotted two scary dogs running into the farmyard. As Beth saw their extra-long teeth and pale wolf-like eyes, she felt very fearful.

The dogs were under Shadow's spell. Storm's enemy had found him!

Without a second thought, Beth raced

into the barn ahead of the dogs. Somehow she knew where Storm would be. Darcy's pen!

She reached the pen at the back of the barn in time to see the tiny black-and-white puppy running into it. As the dogs pursuing Storm ran into the barn, there was a snort of rage and Darcy leaped right over the top bar of the pen and landed on the barn floor.

Braying threateningly, the billy goat ran straight at the fierce dogs with his head lowered. *Bang! Thud!* He butted them in the side, buying Storm precious time.

Suddenly there was a blinding gold flash and bright golden sparks rained down all around Beth and crackled onto the barn floor. Storm was no longer a tiny black-and-white puppy but instead stood before her as a young silver-gray wolf with glowing midnight-blue eyes. At his side was a huge she-wolf with a gentle face.

Beth knew the moment had come when Storm had to leave.

Storm lifted his magnificent head and looked at her with sad eyes. "Be of good heart, Beth. You have been a true friend," he growled in a deep velvety voice. He raised a large silver paw in farewell and then he and his mother faded and were gone.

There was a terrifying howl of rage behind Beth. The dogs' teeth and eyes instantly returned to normal, and they ran out of the barn.

Beth stood alone in the barn. A deep sadness welled up in her. She couldn't believe that Storm had left so suddenly. She was glad he was safe, but she was going to miss him terribly.

"I'll never forget you, Storm," she whispered, her throat closing with tears. She knew that she'd always treasure the time she had shared with the tiny magic puppy.

She heard steps behind her and turned

to see Darcy coming toward her. He leaned forward to nuzzle her arm. "You were really brave. Storm would be so proud of you," she said, petting him before leading him back to his pen. "The sun's coming out. I think I'll ask Aunt Em if you can go out in the field."

Darcy snickered delightedly as if he understood.

"Talking to yourself again?" Martin

joked from behind her. "Are you coming into the farmhouse? I saved you a piece of cake."

As Beth turned to look at her cousin, she grinned. *Trust Martin to have the last word,* she thought, knowing somehow that Storm was watching them, his midnight-blue eyes glowing with approval.

About the Author

Sue Bentley's books for children often include animals, fairies, and wildlife. She lives in Northampton, England, and enjoys reading, going to the movies, relaxing by her garden pond, and watching the birds feeding their babies on the lawn. At school she was always getting yelled at for daydreaming or staring out of the window— but she now realizes that she was storing up ideas for when she became a writer. She has met and owned many cats and dogs, and each one has brought a special kind of magic to her life.

Don't miss these Magic Puppy books!

#1 A New Beginning

#2 Muddy Paws

#3 Cloud Capers

#4 Star of the Show

#5 Party Dreams

#6 A Forest Charm

#7 Twirling Tails

#8 School of Mischief

#9 Classroom Princess

#10 Friendship Forever

#11 Spellbound at School

#12 Sunshine Shimmers

#13 Sparkling Skates

#14 The Perfect Secret

Snowy Wishes

Don't miss these Magic Kitten books!

Don't miss these Magic Ponies books!

Don't miss these Magic Bunny books!

#1 Chocolate Wishes

#2 Vacation Dreams

#3 A Splash of Magic

#4 Classroom Capers

#5 Dancing Days